SOUTHE
Book 2: *The Dirty Side*

Selena Brooks

Southern Sizzle Book 2: The Dirty Side

Written by: Selena Brooks

Published by: Black Authors Rock

Chapter 1

Saniyah was not herself as she prepared her kitchen for another night of service. She had been barking orders at her staff from the moment she hit the door; uncharacteristic of her self-mandated policy of respect and cooperation. Everyone knew something was wrong, but no one had the courage to question the temporary tyrant.

When Ryan arrived at the restaurant, an hour before opening time, Saniyah's displacement of frustration was still in full swing. Her wrath was focused on the food, something she couldn't hurt no matter how strong her attack. She whipped the eggs for her country ham omelets as if they had disobeyed her before moving on to commit assault with a deadly cleaver against the innocent poultry parts that would become her almost-famous fried chicken.

Ryan came into the restaurant through the office in the back of the kitchen. He immediately noticed the unusual quiet coming from the other side of the door between himself and the kitchen. He peeped out to find his chatty, vibrant kitchen team had become a legion of speechless robots. They moved around the kitchen doing their jobs without as much as making eye contact with one another. Ryan struggled to speculate a reason for his staff's new found effectiveness and voyaged out into the kitchen to find the answer. He stopped the first employee he saw, a busy boy named Monty, and requested an explanation.

"Hey, Monty, why's it so quiet in here today?"

Monty seemed reluctant to give his uninformed boss an answer. He looked around and confirmed no other eyes were on him before speaking.

"Chef Saniyah said she don't want to hear no talking…just working." Monty looked around again to assure he hadn't spoken long enough to catch the attention of the kitchen enforcer. He read that Ryan wasn't going to press him for more information so he made a silent retreat toward the sink area.

Ryan didn't recognize Monty's words as something that would come out of Saniyah's mouth so he had to find out for himself. He went in search of Saniyah and found her still chopping away at the helpless chicken. He noticed that the group of assistants usually surrounding her was nowhere in sight. He walked toward her but stopped abruptly when he saw the way she was brutalizing the chicken. He called her name from a distance to get her attention.

Saniyah's whole body tensed at the sound of Ryan's voice. Her grip on the meat cleaver handle tightened before she let it fall onto the prep table. She did not turn to face Ryan but kept her attention focused on the wall in front of her. She waited in harsh silence for him to speak.

Seeing the cleaver leave her hand, Ryan felt it was safe to approach Saniyah. He hesitantly walked toward her. He leaned in to kiss her cheek. Saniyah jerked in the opposite direction of his kiss but not enough to avoid the touch of his lips.

"I'm guessing you still upset about earlier." Ryan correctly assumed.

The apathy in his tone caused Saniyah to break her wall gaze and focus on Ryan's uncaring expression. She did not respond. She simply clutched her weapon of choice and resumed her slaughter of the already-dead chicken. Her retrieval of the sharp object caused Ryan to take a step back.

"So you not speaking to me now?"

The arrogance in his voice irritated Saniyah. He was acting as if the tension between them was unwarranted, and she knew she would have to speak her mind for him to realize the seriousness of what transpired between them.

"Do you really expect me to talk to you after what you did to me?"

"Baby, you know I would never intentionally hurt you." Ryan innocently explained. "I just reacted, and I'm sorry about that."

"Is that lame apology supposed to make me feel better?"

Saniyah was not about to surrender as easily as Ryan had hoped so he pulled out the big, remorseful guns. Ryan got down on both knees and crawled toward Saniyah. He took both of her hands in his and placed a kiss on each fist. Saniyah's first thought was to jerk her hands away, but she decided to play nice and hear him out.

"Niyah, you know I love you with all my heart and I hate myself for causing you pain. I wish that I could take it all back, but I know I can't. I'm just begging you to forgive me, Boo. Give me a second chance. I promise that I will never lay my hands on you ever again."

Although she didn't believe a word that was coming out of his mouth, the love she had for him and his hazel-eyed plea was weakening her bullshit blockade.

"How can I trust you?"

"Because you know I love you just as much as you love me."

"What if love isn't enough to keep you from making the same mistake again?'

"It will."

"How do you know?"

"Because I don't want to die, and I know I can't live without you." Ryan choked on his words as an unfamiliar wetness clouded his vision. He tried to mask his emotions by wiping the tears onto his sleeve, but a single tear escaped him and slid down the side of his face and onto the floor. His unintentional display of vulnerability upset him even more, and he put his leaking head into his hands to smother the unstoppable flow.

Ryan's spiel had bounced off of Saniyah like a rubber ball, but the unanticipated waterworks and masculine whimper had her convinced that he was sincere. It inspired her own display of soggy emotions. She rushed to his side and embraced his balled up frame. He looked up to witness her touch, and she immediately pulled his face into a steamy, tear-soaked kiss.

"So does this mean you forgive me?" Ryan asked as the couple returned to a standing position.

"Yes."

"Do you love me?"

"Of course."

Ryan embraced Saniyah upon her profession of affection. He grabbed her hand and motioned for her to walk with him. She assumed correctly that his aim was to get her back into the office for a make-up quickie. And she was game.

"You not gonna tell anybody about this right?" Ryan requested.

"No. I won't tell anybody about you crying." Saniyah smiled, amused by his boyish insecurity.

"No...I mean you're not gonna tell anybody I put my hands on you, right? You haven't told anyone, have you?"

Ryan scanned their surroundings to see if any of the kitchen employees had witnessed the conversation and was relieved to find they were keeping their distance.

"No." Saniyah replied as confusion engulfed her face. Ryan, on the other hand, was all smiles, and he embraced her once more.

"Good. 'Cause I don't want that out in the street. So keep it to yourself, alright?"

His selfish request reignited Saniyah's previous fears. He hadn't apologized because he was sorry for his actions. He apologized to protect his public image. But instead of calling him out on his exposed intentions, Saniyah defied her own better judgment and drowned her newfound clarity in blind admiration. Her mind was telling her to reject his touch and his phony love, but her heart could not ignore the possibility that her intuition might be wrong.

"Whatever you want, Babe."

Chapter 2

Reese pulled into her apartment complex and parked in her usual spot right next to Andre's Mustang. She cringed at the sight of his pride and joy on wheels; an indication of his presence. She had hoped job searching would have kept him out long enough for her to avoid the dreadful conversation they stood to have about her not-so-immaculate conception for a little while longer.

The pull of guilt tightened in Reese's chest as she continued to stare at Andre's black beauty. The glare of the sun against the car's recently waxed paint job pierced her eyes as if that were its way of showing displeasure with her treatment of its owner. She looked away to avoid the disapproving death ray and plopped her head against her steering wheel. Tears formed in the cracks of her eyes and a strained moan of pain escaped her lips.

"Stupid, stupid, stupid." She muttered, scolding herself and pounding her fists against the dashboard. She closed her eyes to allow the release of the uncontrollable flow of emotion and regret that was building inside; her obscured vision not noticing her unaware lover approaching her vehicle with a smile.

"Hey, Baby." Andre called as he knocked on the window of Reese's car door. His voice startled Reese out of her steering wheel-clutching disposition. Her face was stained with the residue of running mascara. And her attempt to wipe away the evidence of her tears was unsuccessful.

"What's wrong?"

Andre's eyes softened at the sight of his lover's discomfort. He pulled Reese's car door open and reached out to embrace her. She fell into his arms, the warmth of his touch pleasing and torturing her all at once.

"I have something I need to tell you, but I think we should go inside first." Reese choked on her words as she came to grips with what she had to do.

Reese's statement put Andre on high alert and he eased out of their embrace, revealing his premonition on what he was about to hear. He knew whatever it was had to be serious to bring the normally cheerful Reese to tears, and his thoughts were leaning toward his worst fear: Infidelity.

Reese felt the coldness in his release and knew Andre was not emotionally equipped to hear what she had to say. On the ride home, she had fantasized that he would still love her and want to be with her, but the look on his face let her know that would probably not be the reality of the situation. Still, there was the possibility that the child she was carrying was for him and he had the right to know about it.

The couple stood facing one another, examining the expression of their other half. Reese looked away from Andre's stare in shame, fighting back another guilty gush. She walked toward her apartment, and Andre reluctantly followed behind her.

"So what's the deal, Reese?" Andre asked as soon as they were inside her apartment. Reese took notice of his referral to her by first name and not the pet names he usually used. His coldness toward her punctured her heart and the whole truth she had planned to tell him was quickly becoming the half-truth she was going to tell him.

"I'm pregnant!" She blurted before falling onto the couch in tears.

Andre's cold expression faded and he rubbed his forehead in astonishment. He looked down at the weeping mother-to-be and the softness in his eyes returned as it became clear that she was the mother-to-be of *his* child. His astonishment became awe and his shock turned into a smile.

"Baby, that's great!" Andre belted as he gently pulled Reese into his arms and softly pecked her lips.

"It is?" Reese was not expecting his approval. Even though she hadn't told him the other side of the story, she still thought her news would be a hard blow for any unemployed, single man to handle.

"But you're not working, and I'm not making that much at the hotel." Reese reasoned.

"So what?" Andre grinned, not accepting the reality of Reese's statement.

"*So what*? How are we gonna provide for this baby when we barely taking care of ourselves?"

"Don't worry, Boo. I got you…and little Dre."

Andre rubbed Reese's still-firm belly as if it were already poking out. Reese appreciated his caress and compassion, but his answer was unsatisfactory. Their conversation was unveiling the financial difficulty of the situation Reese had managed to overlook while fretting over her two-father dilemma. It also pointed out that a baby for unemployed Andre would carry more of a struggle than a baby for six-figure salary Terrance.

Still, Reese could not move her lips to tell Andre about Terrance. And although the dollar signs that would accompany being Terrance Forrest's baby's momma were appealing, the pain of breaking her best friend's heart far outweighed her love of spending other people's money. So she reluctantly suggested the dreaded obvious solution to all her problems.

"Maybe I should get an abortion."

The nonchalant tone of her voice shocked them both. Reese, the daughter of a devout Catholic mother, knew the sin of her suggestion and was not even sure she could go through with it. Andre, the son of two on-again, off-again Baptists, on the other hand, was just enraged at the thought of his seed being murdered. He grabbed Reese's arms firmly and stared at her as if she were the most awkward thing he had ever seen.

"Why would you even fix your mouth to say that to me?" Andre scolded as he released her from his grasp.

"I just don't think we're ready for this baby, Dre." Reese explained rubbing her slightly irritated arms.

"Well, let me show you how ready *I* am." Andre fell down on one knee without warning. He clutched both of Reese's hands and looked directly up into her eyes.

"Reese, will you marry me?" His smile revealed those dimples that no woman could dare refuse.

"What?" Reese blurted. Andre knew the queen of non-commitment would not come around easily and was prepared for her resistance.

"I want you to know just how much you and this baby mean to me. I want both of you in my life forever. I want us to be a family."

Reese's eyes filled with tears for the fourth time that day. Tears that should have been blended with joy were laced with uncertainty. The sincerity of his proposal showed how much he truly cared for not only her, but also the baby inside her – whom he'd only known about for five minutes. But it also made her realize that the feelings she held for him would never be that deep. As she fell into the depths of indecision, her faucet of emotion sprayed even harder. Andre misinterpreted the feelings behind her tears and used them as motivation to continue his proposal speech.

"I know that I'm broke and jobless right now, but I put it on my life that I will do everything in my power to make sure you and little Dre are

well taken care of….so will you marry me?"

Reese could not bring herself to deny

Andre's heartfelt plea. So she shouted out the exact

opposite of what she was thinking with a forced

smile.

"Yes!"

Chapter 3

Ryan and Saniyah cuddled on the sofa admiring the white glow of the lights on the fake pine Christmas tree they had just finished decorating. The sounds of Donny Hathaway's "This Christmas" soothed their ears, and the infusion of the bourbon-laced eggnog Saniyah had prepared from scratch mellowed their posture with every sip.

The couple sat in the blissful, silent warmth of their embrace, appreciating every moment of their first Christmas Eve together. To their parents' dismay, they had decided to spend their holiday at home. They didn't want to attempt the feat of trying to travel to both Mobile and Meridian -

where Ryan's mother had recently relocated - in one day.

Tomorrow, they would exchange gifts and share a quiet dinner - which Saniyah would spend all Christmas morning preparing - with Reese and Andre. But tonight was all theirs and they planned to savor the time they had without the usual interruptions about restaurant or club issues.

Ryan flipped the channel on his television from the "Christmas Movie" marathon they were no longer interested in to his electronic fire place scene. A fantasy of playing Santa and Mrs. Claus with his now-tipsy companion was stirring in his head and he wanted to set the romantic tone. He leaned into Saniyah and breathed in the familiar scent of fresh flowers and lavender that perfumed her neck and chest. He pressed his lips against her neck and allowed the tip of his tongue to moisten the territory. But just as his hand was about to slip under her skirt, she gripped his arm and brought their holiday hump fest to a screeching halt.

He pulled his mouth away from her body long enough to whine.

"What's wrong, Baby?"

"We need to talk."

Ryan's sex pose fell into a frustrated, arm-folded slump as he realized Saniyah was not in the mindset for any Christmas Eve nookie. And his analysis of her thoughts could not have been more right. There was something she had been dying to share with him for a while, but the right opportunity had never come. They both seemed to always be busy at work, stressed from work, or working each other in the bedroom. Conversations between them were few and usually revolved around business. So she saw this work-free, stress-free moment as the perfect time to get her thoughts off her chest.

"What you wanna talk about?" Ryan huffed.

"Well, I've been thinking about opening my own restaurant." Saniyah's eyes lit up as she made her career ambitions known. And she paid little attention to the disposition of her disgruntled lover.

"Your own restaurant? But you already have a restaurant...*our* restaurant." Ryan reasoned. Saniyah had never heard Ryan refer to the Boiling Point as *"our"* restaurant. She appreciated his attempt to share ownership, but that one reference matched against thousands of others to the contrary made the insincerity behind his comment obvious.

"No, baby, that is *your* restaurant...*your* vision." Saniyah corrected.

"I thought it was *our* vision." Ryan contradicted. His continued undermining of her effort to have an independent goal irritated her. In the countless times she had envisioned the outcome of this conversation in her head, he had been a perfect, encouraging version of himself. But it was becoming apparent that the real Ryan was not willing to overlook his own selfish needs to support her dream.

Saniyah knew an argument was brewing inside their conversation; an argument that could lead to another vicious attack from her volatile companion. She did not want to risk another violent episode. So she got up from the sofa and prepared to make an exit before the tone turned sour.

"Where you goin'?" Ryan asked, softly grasping Saniyah's wrist to impede her movement. His gentle touch kept Saniyah from pulling away.

"It's obvious that you're not planning to be open-minded and hear me out, and I don't feel like arguing with you on Christmas Eve. So I'm going to bed." Saniyah freed her arm from his grasp and started to make her way toward the bedroom.

"C'mon, Saniyah. You expect me to be happy about my chef making plans to abandon me?" Ryan got up from the sofa and walked in Saniyah's direction. Although he had a slight smile on his face, his approach and the content of their conversation made Saniyah take a few steps back. Nervously, she muttered.

"Who said I was planning to abandon you?"

"You really think you gonna be able to manage running my kitchen and opening your own place at the same time?"

"Well, I haven't thought of all the details, but you could at least be supportive while I figure it out."

"It's hard for me to support an idea when I know there's no way it's gonna happen."

Although his expression of absolute negativity was not surprising, the pure ease with which he spat it out with no regard for her feelings baffled Saniyah.

"Wow. You have absolutely no faith in my ability to stand on my own."

The conversation was beginning to resemble the countless cooking school arguments she had been through with her mother. And just as she had won those arguments and become a successful chef, she planned to notch another victory and become an even more successful restaurateur.

"It's not that I don't have faith in you, Boo. It's just that I don't have faith in what you're trying to do. And I know once you take some time to think about it, you'll see that I'm right."

Saniyah realized that Ryan Taylor planned to be a much worthier opponent than Alice Walker had been in the defeat and destruction of her cuisine-based dreams, especially when he believed those dreams were working against the advancement of his own ambitions. But she refused to bend to the will of her egomaniacal, on-the-verge-of-becoming-an-ex boyfriend, and she knew the debate between them would go on and on until her surrender was the outcome.

Without another word, Saniyah redirected her path in the opposite direction. She swiftly made her way to the front door and was turning the knob before Ryan fixed his mouth to object.

"Where you think you going now?" He pressed her for information that he was obviously not going to receive.

"Away from you."

Saniyah pulled the door open and exited, slamming it shut behind her. Ryan cringed at the sight and sound of the bells attached to the Christmas wreath banging violently against the door and clanging out an un-jolly jingle. Saniyah's newfound dominance had quieted her oppressor, but his silence was short lived. Ryan was not one to yield the last word to anyone. So as the clop of Saniyah's high-heeled footsteps got farther away, he hurled one last insulting blow.

"Well Merry-fucking Christmas to you, too!"

Andre leaned against the thin, white column between himself and Reese's front door. He inhaled the smoke from a newly-lit Newport cigarette and released the cancerous puff into the cool winter air. The stress of nonexistent interviews

and soon-to-be-overdue bills had inspired the
addictive habit that kept him outdoors more than he
liked, especially with an abnormal cold front
moving in and dropping temperatures to 20 degrees.
He saw chill bumps forming on his uncovered arms
and knew it wouldn't be long before he retreated
inside to the warmth of the apartment. He rubbed
his arms to provide temporary relief and extend his
nicotine fix a little longer.

When his cigarette had burned down to the
Newport logo, he knew it was ready to be
extinguished so he dropped it onto the pavement
and crushed its burn under the sole of his Adidas
flip flop. Before he turned to walk back inside the
apartment, he noticed a familiar car pulling into the
complex. As the vehicle got closer, he recognized it
as Saniyah's Honda. Reese hadn't mentioned that
her cousin would be visiting, and from the content

of the phone conversation he had with Ryan earlier that day, he knew the couple was planning to spend some alone time together that night. He knew something had to be wrong for Saniyah to be coming over at 11:30 at night on Christmas Eve when she was supposed to be with her man being more naughty than nice. So even with his chill bumps begging for mercy, he decided to greet her at the door and find out what was going on.

A few moments after parking her car and turning off the ignition, Saniyah exited the vehicle and shut the door a little harder than normal. Her heels clicked out a determined stride as she made her way to the underdressed figure standing between herself and her cousin's threshold. As she moved closer, the figure became the familiar physique she still secretly desired. The after smell of a recent cigarette break filled her nostrils. She

twisted her face in disgust at the unpleasant aroma.

"Ugh. You been smoking?" She asked

before the sight of a freshly-flattened butt on the

walkway answered her question.

"Yeah. You got a problem with it?" Andre

huffed, folding his arms to show his indifference for

whatever her answer would be.

"If you wanna kill yourself, go right ahead."

Saniyah snapped. Her harsh comment put Andre on

the defensive. He had heard the "kill yourself"

speech from Reese and his father since developing

the habit and he was in no mood to listen to

anymore lectures from gainfully employed,

successful people who did not understand his plight.

"Why are you here?" Andre redirected the

conversation to the subject he was dying to hear

about. The chilled breaths that carried his words

made Saniyah notice his white wife beater and black basketball shorts -- less than appropriate attire for the current weather. She also noticed his intent to pry and used her observation as a means to avoid his interrogation.

"You not cold?"

"Answer my question."

"Reese here?"

"Maybe."

"Boy, is my cousin here or not?"

"I'll answer your question only if you answer mine."

Saniyah ignored his comment and started for the door, but Andre pressed his body into the door frame to block her entry. She tried to alert her cousin to her presence by ringing the doorbell, but Andre playfully swatted her hand away. She reached for the doorknob, but he blocked it with his arm. Her irritation with Andre's immaturity added to the frustration of her fight with Ryan and inspired an outburst of tearful emotion she had been holding in since storming out of his apartment.

The smile Andre had been wearing since beginning his game of keep away faded into concern.

"Damn, Niyah, don't cry. I was gonna let you in eventually." He half joked, half consoled as he reached his arm around her shoulders to comfort her.

"Well, I'm not in the mood for your games. Me and Ryan had a fight, and I need to talk to Reese." She whimpered, wiping her eyes with her sleeve as her downpour calmed to a trickle.

"Did he hit you?" Andre blurted. He had bailed Ryan out of jail once before for putting his hands on a past female acquaintance, but his best friend had assured his abusive ways were behind

him. Andre didn't want to unnecessarily alarm

Saniyah if their disagreement hadn't come to blows

and be responsible for putting his homeboy's past

indiscretions on blast. He wished he could take the

revealing comment back, but the surprised look on

Saniyah's face let him know it could not be

retracted.

"No." Saniyah lied, partly to keep the

promise she made to protect her abuser's image and

partly to protect herself from the embarrassment she

stood to feel if her strong-willed cousin found out

how lenient she had been. She reasoned to herself

that Ryan hadn't hit her in their latest fight so her

lie was only halfway untrue.

Andre read the discomfort in her posture and

the intent to deceive in her tone, but without seeing

any physical signs of abuse, he could only take her

at her word. He gave her a sympathetically aware

gaze hoping it would let her know that when she

was ready to be honest she could confide in him.

He released her from his embrace and opened the

door.

"Reese is in the bedroom." Andre informed.

"You want me to get her for you?"

Saniyah nodded once she was inside. The

warm air in the festively-decorated living room

eased her freezing body as she adjusted to the

temperature change.

Andre went to revive his sleeping beauty

with a not-so-charming nudge to the shoulder. She

muttered something that sounded like "I'm gonna

kick your ass," before finally rising from her

interrupted slumber. Since accepting his proposal,

everything her incompatible fiancé did, outside of

supplying her cravings and massaging her feet, irritated her.

"Saniyah's here. She and Ryan had a fight and she's pretty upset." The mere mention of her favorite cousin being present *and* upset squashed Reese's desire to fall back into bed and sent her scrambling for the living room.

Before long, the trio was lounging on the couch discussing the argument over marshmallow-filled cups of hot cocoa. Saniyah told about her desire to have her own restaurant and how Ryan had shot her idea down like a skeet shooter.

"Girl, you've got too much talent to be wasting on somebody else's kitchen forever. If you feel ready to move on and do your own thing, I say go for it. And if Ryan can't handle it, FUCK HIM!" Reese encouraged, her almost-inspirational rant and out-of-whack hormones had sweat beads running down her neck. She wiped them away with her palm and immediately went in search of the thermostat in the hallway to lower the temperature.

Saniyah saw Reese's absence as an opportunity to find out Andre's true feelings on the issue, being that his best friend was on the other side of the disagreement.

"I saw you nodding your head agreeing with your fiancée, but Ryan is your boy. So what you really think about me leaving his restaurant to get my own spot?"

"Honestly, the way you cook, you could serve that shit out a cardboard box and be a success. Hell, you *are* the Boiling Point, but if you feel like the Boiling Point ain't you, then, in my opinion, you gotta move on." Andre's words of encouragement fed her starving ego and she was craving more.

"So you really think my restaurant will be a success?"

"If I had the money, I'd fund the whole thing...Matter of fact...now that I think of it...there is a way I can help you out."

"What you got fifty grand stashed away somewhere?" Saniyah joked before remembering his unemployed, broke, baby-on-the-way situation and regretting her comment.

"No, but I may be able to get you some investors and a building all in one package."

His proposal caught Saniyah's attention and she traded her sarcasm for intrigue.

"How?"

"My dad owns a construction company. He mainly builds office buildings and outlet malls, but I'm sure he could handle a restaurant. Shit, I may be able to get him to do it for free. We just have to

find you a good deal on some land."

The word "free" rang in Saniyah's frugal

head.

"Free? Are you serious?"

"I wouldn't have said it if I wasn't. I can

holler at him about it tomorrow if you want and get

him to round up his rich friends looking for a new

investment. Are you interested?"

Andre had Saniyah's future planned out in a

matter of minutes, and she was impressed by his

eagerness to take charge and get things done. But

in all of this new information being revealed about

her savvy friend, one question was burning her

curiosity.

"Andre, why are you unemployed? I mean

your dad owns his own company." Saniyah blurted

without concern for the personal nature of the

information she was requesting. Her question
snapped Andre out of his business dream and back
into his jobless reality. He pondered how to answer
her question and came to a simple response.

"I want something that's mine. He helps me
out when I need it, but I wanna make my own way."

His words were reflective of her own
journey to break away from her parents' clutches of
fiscal control over her life so she needed no further
explanation. She admired and empathized with his
determination and the way he was sticking to it
even at a time when his father's support would be a
rescue blanket. And she was beginning to
appreciate the similarities of his character to her
own.

"Are you interested or not?"

"You think you can make all that happen?"

"Of course."

"Okay, Partner."

"*Partner*?"

"You expect me to accept all these favors from you and not have your back? I cook, you manage. Do we have a deal?"

Saniyah stuck out her right hand awaiting his grasp in acceptance of her proposal.

"Deal!"

Before he even had a chance to think, Andre grabbed her hand and a partnership was brought into the world on the Eve of Christ's birth. And it couldn't have been more heaven sent for Andre, who was beginning to think he would never work again. He understood it would take some time and effort before the profit of his labor would be realized. But he couldn't shake the feeling that the restaurant deal could be his only chance to have the success he craved. With Reese not due for another five months, he knew he could have plenty of money rolling in soon enough to conquer the financial demands of parenthood.

Just as the two released their contractual shake, Reese returned to the living room biting into a green Christmas-tree shaped sugar cookie. A sudden craving for something sweet had delayed her return with a trip through the kitchen in hot pursuit of the holiday-themed treats. And she had eaten all but one of the six cookies she had pulled out of the bag before making it back into the living room.

The closeness between Saniyah and Andre alerted Reese that her absence had not gone without some conversation she was determined to know about.

"What I miss?" She muffled through the crunch of cookie crumbs.

Not wanting to upset Momzilla, Andre and Saniyah willingly filled her in on the details of their discussion. But in the calm that followed Reese's loud outburst of congratulations, hugs, and kisses, Saniyah remembered she still needed a place to sleep. There was no way in Hell she was going back to Ryan's place anytime soon, maybe *ever* after the way he had disrespected her dream.

       She knew Reese had the extra room that she once called her own, but she didn't want to impose on their Christmas Eve any more than she already had. So she pulled herself up from her cousin's cozy couch and prepared for the cruel cold she would face searching for a hotel room.

       "Okay, well, I guess I better go try to find a room for the night."

       "*A room*?" Reese squeaked.

       "You know I'm not going back to Ryan's."

"Girl, please. I ain't even about to let my favorite cousin spend Christmas Eve in no hotel. As long as I got a roof over my head, so do you."

Chapter 4

Reese pulled her small suitcase down the corridor leading to the American Airlines baggage claim in the biggest airport she had ever been to. As she walked, she took in its enormity, imagining how the entire Gulfport airport she had flew out of could probably fit in one of this airport's bathrooms. Her stomach fluttered with anxiety and anticipation for what her trip would hold as she got closer to her destination.

After what seemed like an eternity lugging her overstuffed carry on, Reese reached the baggage claim area in time to see her checked suitcase make its second trip around the conveyor belt. She hurried to retrieve it before it started on its third go round, which turned out to be a more difficult task than she had anticipated. She had spent the entire previous night packing outfits and accessories for every occasion she thought might come up on her two-day trip. So her effort to lift the crammed luggage was a struggle until the burden of her task was relieved by a masculine, Caucasian hand.

"Let me help you with that." The unknown man said as he hoisted her suitcase from the conveyor belt with ease and sat it down in front of her.

"Thank you so much." Reese praised her savior with a smile. The glare of sunlight on his silver name tag displaying "Joseph Hinds" followed by "Sanitation Department" drew her attention from his flushed, wrinkled face to his overworked, beer-belly toting torso.

"Always my pleasure to help out a pretty lady." He said with a slight smile that revealed a hint of his yellow-stained teeth. On his breath was the faint smell of nicotine that reminded Reese of Andre's unattractive new habit. She freed her mind of the boyfriend she had left behind as she grabbed the handle of her luggage and prepared to make an exit that her new acquaintance was not ready to allow.

"So where you coming in from?" He asked. He had noticed the unfamiliarity of her accent.

"Mississippi." Reese replied, knowing from past experience that mention of her home city alone would not be enough information to satisfy his inquiry.

"Ah, the hospitality state." He said, shaking his head with recognition.

"Yep. That's right." She said with an irritated smile, wishing the small talk with the man she never planned to know would come to an end.

He correctly interpreted her shortness and brought their conversation to a fitting finish with his next comment.

"Well, Miss Mississippi, let me be the first to welcome you to the city of Dallas." He said with a smile that beamed with the pride he held for his place of residence. "I hope you enjoy your stay."

"Thanks." She replied with a nod that signaled her exit and the end of the conversation. Without another word, both parties moved in different directions and out of each other's lives for good.

Reese reached the front entrance of Dallas-Fort Worth International Airport in time to hear the chirp of a text message on her cell phone. She retrieved the device from the back pocket of her jeans and found the message was from her absent host, Terrance. It apologized for his tardiness and explained that he was stuck in traffic and would be there shortly. Reese was slightly annoyed by his obvious lack of planning-ahead skills, but her growing need to relieve her feet of the ache from the four-inch stiletto boots she was wearing erased all other thoughts and sent her in search of a resting place.

When Terrance pulled his brand new black Camaro into the arrivals lane twenty minutes later, Reese was parked on a bench two seconds away from taking the boots off of her swelling feet. He noticed his unmistakably beautiful lover immediately and pulled his chrome-trimmed, 20-inch rim-fitted chariot right in front of where she was sitting. The dark tint of his windows prevented Reese from seeing who was inside.

As he exited the car and revealed his identity to the outside world, a taxi driver yelled to him from his cab window.

"Hey, T, how 'bout them Cowboys next year?"

"All the way!" He spits out his rehearsed, overused answer without hesitation. His perfect smile was filled with confidence as he waved his index finger in the air signaling the ranking his underperforming, out-of-the-playoff-picture team would need to get to the Super Bowl.

The carry of his unique baritone played in Reese's ear and alerted her to his presence. She looked up from the task of removing her boots and was greeted by his grey-eyed grace walking toward her. He walked right up to her and pulled her into an unexpected embrace followed by the soft press of his kiss upon her cheek. The familiar scent of his cologne reignited the fire of her desire for him that melted the chill in the wintry winds blowing in from the snowy Northwest.

The pair held their embrace and gazed into each other's eyes, relishing the joy of their long-anticipated reunion. Memories of their Beau Rivage rendezvous filled their minds, and they simultaneously hoped the new encounter would have similar results. But Reese's hopes were slightly compromised by the revelation she would have to make before the trip came to an end. Her flutters of anxiety returned and caused her to ease out of Terrance's embrace.

"You okay?" He inquired.

"Yeah, Baby. I'm fine, just a little tired from the flight." She lied, trying to conceal her uneasiness with a fake smile.

"Do you wanna go to the hotel and rest for a minute?" He suggested as he went to retrieve her luggage.

"*Hotel*? I thought I was staying with you."

The new information put Reese on high alert and her mind started doing flips as she searched for a reason why a single, successful man would not invite his female guest to stay at his place.

"Well, the owner of my condo decided he wanted to repaint the place at the last minute, and I didn't want you sucking in fumes all weekend so I got us a suite at the Renaissance."

His answer left Reese feeling unsure about its credibility. Terrance read the uncertainty on her face and made an attempt to ease her mind while loading her belongings into his trunk.

"Don't worry, Baby. You'll get to see it in all of its freshly-painted glory next time I get you out here."

"How you know it's gonna *be* a next time?"

A sly smile crept across Terrance's face as he slammed his trunk shut.

"Cause I'mma beat it up so good this time, you won't wanna leave."

The blunt aggressiveness in his response reminded Reese of how much his bedroom dominance turned her on. A yearning throb built between her thighs, and she knew whether it happened at his place or in a hotel room was no longer relevant. She was ready to have him inside her as soon as possible, wherever possible.

"Well, why we still standing here?" Reese pressed. "Let's go."

Terrance and Reese pulled into the front entrance that sat directly below the towering rise of the Renaissance Dallas Hotel. The architectural brilliance of the luxury hotel's sleek design impressed Reese. And her fondness for the hotel's elegance grew even more once inside.

Only two days after Christmas had come and gone, the spirit of the holiday was still alive and well in the merry décor of the lobby. The glimmer of lights and the shine of the gold, red, and green spheres hanging from enormous Christmas trees were a beautiful sight to behold. Reese couldn't help thinking about how the room's immaculate trappings put the Oasis' small tinsel-drowned tree to shame.

The couple walked through the lobby hand-in-hand, catching the admiring stares of hotel guests and employees familiar with Terrance's work.

Reese was beginning to like the attention his celebrity status attracted. But in the back of her mind, she hoped her being seen with him would not thrust the details of their private affair into the public and reach the ears and eyes back home.

To Reese's surprise, their stroll of significance led them past the front desk and straight to the elevators.

"Don't we need to check in, Sweetie?"

"Already taken care of." Terrance responded, pulling a hotel key card from the side pocket of his slacks.

"Well, aren't we prepared?" Reese teased.

"Always, Boo."

"You sure wasn't prepared for that traffic on the way to get me."

"But I got your ass."

"Yeah, you got me. *Twenty minutes late,* but you got me."

"Hey, Girl, you keep popping off at the mouth and Daddy gonna have to spank you." Terrance chastised her with a playful grin.

"Maybe I like to be spanked."

At her words, the doors of the elevator opened and Terrance's manhood hardened. He pulled her into the elevator and was about to lock her up in a passionate kiss until he noticed the tiny, elderly Mexican woman who had slipped into the elevator unnoticed. She smiled at the couple, amused by their youthful passion and by the stranglehold her presence had put on their romantic exchange. They both returned fake innocent smiles they hoped would hide their desperate need for fornication.

The elevator stopped on the fourth floor, and the elderly woman prepared to exit. She gave the couple one last knowing smile.

"You kids have fun tonight." She said as she walked out into the hallway.

The couple smiled in awe of her foreshadowing comment and broke into laughter once the elevator doors had closed. The laughter calmed their raging hormones, and they managed to make it inside their suite without any sexual contact.

Reese was impressed with Terrance's choice of accommodations for their weekend getaway. Their executive suite had a separate living area, bar, and dining area, two 42-inch flat-screen TVs, a king-sized bed with pillow-top mattress and a breath-taking view of the downtown Dallas skyline that would be ten times better once the sun went down. Terrance was immediately drawn to the bar

and went to explore the selections it had to offer.

He pulled out two cocktail glasses and was about to

fill them with Hennessy and Coke before Reese

stopped him.

"You don't have to fix one for me. I'm not

drinking tonight."

"And why is that?"

"Because I wanna know what you feel like

sober."

Her flirt was only half true, with the other

reason for her sobriety being the well-being of his

possible unborn child he knew nothing about. But

her deception went undetected, and the sexiness of

her sultry, southern accent mixed with the content

of her comment sent Terrance's hormones right

back into hyper drive. He abandoned the bar

without a drink, intending to find a better use for his hands and mouth.

The couple engaged in an exchange of spastic kisses. Reese managed to stay connected to her partner's lips as she maneuvered her body out of her black leather jacket and slung it to the floor. She yanked Terrance's long-sleeved dress shirt out of his pants and began to unfasten the buttons. To her dismay, the removal of his shirt revealed the added obstacle of an all-white wife beater between herself and his perfect pecs. She pulled the undershirt up as far as it would go and massaged the crevices of his bulging back and chiseled chest.

Terrance snatched the belt out of the loops on Reese's jeans and unzipped them. He discarded the belt to the floor and slid his hands between denim fabric and voluptuous curves. He gripped her behind firmly before releasing her kiss to slide her jeans down to her ankles. His return up ended halfway as he stopped to remove her pink, lace-trimmed boy shorts. He massaged her femininity and she purred her approval; a purr that grew into a growl when he replaced his hand with his mouth. He used his tongue with the precision of surgeon's scalpel as he dissected her, and she grabbed onto his head with both hands to steady and guide his incisions.

Terrance continued to inspect her insides until he felt her leg twitching out a signal of her approaching climax. He eased his tongue out of her to keep her from experiencing an early eruption. He wanted his organ to make her sing the concluding bars of their love song. So he returned to a standing position and lifted her legs around his waist. He carried her over to the bar and sat her down on an unoccupied spot. He removed her blouse to reveal an uncharacteristic bulge in her belly. He remembered her having a practically washboard stomach in their earlier experience but assumed her growth was the result of too many helpings over the holidays.

As Terrance kissed Reese's neck and chest, he felt the uncomfortable press of his wallet in his side pocket coming between himself and the bar. He pulled the wallet from his pocket and remembered the single condom it held. He and Reese hadn't used protection last time, but he figured it was worth a mention. He kissed from her neck to her earlobe and whispered an airy inquiry into her ear.

"You think we ought to use protection this time?"

"No. I don't want nothing coming between us."

Reese knew she already had the ultimate birth control.

Terrance's own desire for unobstructed passion was ignited by her comment, but her willingness to forgo safety and risk fertilization intrigued him. He was just about to probe further into her reasoning when Reese took it upon herself to end the pleasure-pausing conversation. She unzipped his pants, reached into his boxers, and freed his swell from captivity. She massaged him better than he could ever imagine doing for himself, and all other thoughts vanished from his mind. The speed of her aggressive stroke increased with every motion, and when the intensity was too much for him to handle, his body jerked involuntarily causing him to slip out of her grasp.

"*Uh Uh.* Don't run...*Handle it!*" She demanded, using his past domineering words against him. But this time around, the comment had the opposite effect. Instead of inspiring him to submit to her, it motivated him to recapture control of the situation.

He pulled the legs of his unsuspecting victim forward causing her to fall backward onto the bar. He spread her thighs and penetrated her walls with stealth force, trying his best to poke a hole in her stomach with every thrust. He held her arms down to steady her imprisonment in his stroke. The only times he released his hold were to deliver the sporadic spanks he had promised would be the result of her bad behavior.

Reese writhed in the Heaven and Hell she was simultaneously experiencing. Up until that point, she didn't believe he could repeat -- let alone outdo -- his previous powerful performance. But he proved her wrong with every stroke, every poke,

every spank, and every "Whose is this?" he
rendered her unable to answer.

His thrust had her powerless and speechless
but not thoughtless. And her mind was consumed
by an epiphany as his body delivered a final back-
stiffening, toe-curling blow to her system. Not only
did she want this man; she wanted *only* this man.
No other lover would ever be able to fulfill her
needs the way he did. And their connection was
one she had yet to feel with the fiancé she hadn't
thought about once since seeing Terrance again.

Her feelings for him were not quite love, but
more than the mere lust she felt with all the other
men in her past. And the way Terrance pleased her
made it unmistakably clear that it was God's
original plan for their bodies *and* hearts to
eventually be one. She still did not have it in her to
end her one-sided relationship with Andre on her

own. So she secretly prayed for DNA to do her

dirty work.

"Lord, I know this is selfish, but can you

please make the baby inside me a Forrest and not a

Sullivan?"

Chapter 5

Reese awoke the next morning from her sex-induced stupor and found the other side of her cozy cradle abandoned. She rubbed the silk sheets underneath the disheveled comforter and discovered no warmth from recent body heat. Wherever Terrance was, he had been there for a while. She called his name and her echo rang throughout the vast space of the suite. Her call went unanswered.

The inner workings of her mind immediately went the negative route as she imagined every bad situation possible that could be responsible for his absence. Her nerves mixed with the steak she had devoured at dinner and sent her fumbling for the bathroom. She and Terrance had managed to pull themselves together after their bar-top bash and make the dinner reservation he had set up for them at Pappadeaux's Seafood Kitchen. And she was paying the price for the late meal.

When Reese came out from spilling her guts in the bathroom, she found Terrance still hadn't returned. She tried to find the positive in his absence and decided to use the alone time to sort through her feelings about their situation. Last night, Terrance's sex drive had her ready to abandon everything she had ever known and start a whole new life with him in Texas.

But as her reasonable mind had returned, she knew she couldn't base her baby's future on the man that could please her the most sexually. It was obvious that Terrance could provide a stable home and comfortable lifestyle. But what wasn't clear about her acquaintance of only five months was if he had the ability to provide the love and attention a child needed from both parents.

Reese realized that Andre might never have the ability to provide her and her child with everything they wanted, but she knew he was the type of person to try to do it anyway. And from her own experience with him, she knew he would treat her and the baby with the utmost love and respect even when they did not return the favor. So when Terrance walked back into the room carrying their luggage and a bag of Dunkin Donuts, she had made her choice.

Reese wore an uneasy smile as Terrance stowed their bags in the closet and walked towards her holding her Coach purse as far away from his body as he could manage. His outstretched arm brought the $400 bag right up to her face and dropped it softly into her lap.

"Somebody been blowing your phone up, Boo. It rang like six times since I came back from the parking garage." Terrance informed.

Reese had forgotten all about her purse and phone being left inside of his trunk with the rest of her bags. The events of the previous night had distracted her mind from everything else. She quickly retrieved the phone from the inside pocket of her purse and checked her missed calls. The display let her know she had missed thirty calls and had new voicemail messages. Further investigation showed her that Andre was the culprit responsible for the majority of the onslaught of calls. He had called her twenty-seven of the thirty times her phone went unanswered.

"Damn, you got that nigga whipped!" Terrance teased as he glanced over her shoulder and peeped out the screen displaying "Andre (27)."

"I recall you blowing my phone up a time or two when you were trying to get me to come visit you."

"Yeah, yeah, yeah, but it worked. Didn't it?" Terrance boasted.

Reese could only laugh at the truth of his comment, but the laughter did not relieve the nerves building inside her from the sight of all the missed calls from her fiancé. She knew he was probably upset that she did not answer and may have been becoming suspicious of her actions. Although she did not want to face the flack, she knew he was about to give her, she pressed the send button to return one of his many calls.

As it began to ring, she whispered a warning to Terrance, who was sitting in the chair across from her position on the edge of the bed about to inhale a jelly-filled doughnut.

"Please be quiet while I'm on the phone with him." She pleaded.

Terrance nodded to signal his agreement with her request as he stuffed his face with the calorie-riddled pastry his trainer would've slapped out of his mouth had he been there.

"What the fuck is wrong with you, Girl? I been worried sick about you all night. Why haven't you answered any of my calls?" Andre's voice blasted through the speaker without warning. Reese pulled the phone away from her ear to reduce the sting.

"I'm sorry, Baby. I forgot to turn my phone back on after I got off the plane." Reese gave a lie-tainted apology.

"And you didn't think to call me once and let me know you had made it and were alright?"

"I've been busy."

"Busy doing what?"

"You know my Aunt Terry is sick, Boo. I've been spending all my time helping her."

Andre suddenly felt guilty about the verbal assault he had planted on his wife-to-be. His rage had made him forget that she told him she was going to visit her great aunt – a recent victim of a serious stroke. According to Reese, her Aunt Terry, from her father's side of the family, had become paralyzed on her entire left side and needed assistance at all times.

"Oh. I'm sorry, Boo. I forgot about that." Andre calmed his voice to a soft, apologetic tone.

"It's okay, Baby. You have the right to be upset with me. I should've remembered to call so you wouldn't be worried."

"So how is your aunt doing?"

"She was up and down yesterday, but she's cool now." Reese lied. What Andre did not know was that Reese's sick Aunt "Terry" was actually her very healthy man on the side, who was being more than amused by the fabrication in their conversation.

"*Aunt Terry?*" Terrance whispered, trying to hold back a laugh. Reese cracked a smile at the absurdity of her tall tale and put a finger to her lip to remind him of her need for silence.

"So how's my baby doing?" Andre changed his tone again, this time to a sweet, romantic lull.

"I'm fine."

"I meant my other baby."

"Oh." Reese was not yet prepared to alert Terrance, who was immersed in her conversation, to the fact that she was pregnant so she chose her next words carefully and kept her reply simple.

"Everything is cool."

"Good. That's all I wanted to hear. You know I love ya'll too much for you to not be answering the phone, Girl. I was about to fly to Dallas."

"I know. I love you, too." Reese tried to hide the discomfort his words had caused and shake the image of him flying to Dallas and discovering her wrongdoings. But she did appreciate the words of endearment for her and her child.

Terrance, on the other hand, did not appreciate the affection in Reese's words and was becoming jealous of the man whose voice was taking up the time he wanted to spend with her. He decided to take it upon himself to cut short the conversation Reese was not ending fast enough.

He walked over to her and knelt down in front of her curious face. He leaned into her and began to caress the side of her neck with his mouth and tongue, causing a subtle sigh of pleasure to escape her lips. She sealed her mouth with her free hand, praying Andre had not heard her. She removed her hand, once she felt it was moan-free, and grabbed Terrance's mouth to force him away. But Terrance was not about to let her terminate his mission. So he took two of her fingers in his mouth and began to suck them like a kid eating a popsicle.

Reese almost dropped the phone. She knew it was time to end the conversation and sought the words to wrap it up before Terrance found something else to suck.

"Baby, my aunt needs me. Can I call you back later?" Reese managed to push the words out and hold back her desire to murmur Terrance's name.

"Yeah, that's cool…"

"Bye." Reese blurted and ended the call before he could respond. She dropped the phone on the bed beside her and replaced the fingers in his mouth with a ravenous kiss. She used her lips to guide Terrance further onto the bed and fell back to support his weight on top of her.

Without warning, Terrance brought their suck fest to a screeching halt and looked down into Reese's eyes the same way he stared down linebackers who got in his way. His expression scared Reese and she almost had to look away from the glare.

"What's wrong, Baby?" She whined. Her feminine voice and mild eyes softened his expression.

"What I gotta do for you to tell *me* you love me?" Reese didn't know how to respond to his impromptu inquiry so she blurted out words she immediately regretted.

"I do love you, Terrance…"

"But not as much as Andre." He interrupted, finishing her sentence with words she had not planned on using. She knew the opposite was true, but she kept her feelings quiet. Her silence influenced Terrance to lift off of her and scoot back down to sit on the edge of the bed. Reese lifted up behind him but remained in her spot in the middle of the bed to keep a cautious distance between them.

"*Wow*! You really wanna be with that broke ass, no-job having, Bama-ass nigga over *me*?" He fumed.

"Don't talk about him like that?" Reese scolded his immature criticism. "You don't know him enough to be saying that!"

Terrance's back was facing his pad-less opponent, and before he spoke, he looked back at her so she could feel the intensity of his words.

"I know that nigga's standing between me and my lady." Had his comment come at another time, Reese would have been flattered and turned on by his reference to her being his *"lady."* But the content of their current situation was becoming too heated for flattery or romance.

"Well, you also knew me and him were together before we started seeing each other. So why you got a problem with it now?" Reese snapped. She didn't know why she was getting so angry and tried to calm her heavy breathing as she waited for his response.

"Because ever since I met you, I wanted to have you to myself. And since I found out you had a man, it's been my plan to make you leave him."

Terrance's voice was pained and the sincerity in his words made Reese's eyes mist.

"But I can't." She choked out, wiping her tears and swallowing her emotion.

"Why not? Why would you want fish when you can have lobster?" He threw his hands up in frustration.

"Because that fish is my fiancé." Reese finally spoke the truth about the seriousness of her relationship with Andre.

"I don't see no ring on your finger." Terrance had immediately directed his attention to the unoccupied ring finger on her right hand and figured she was lying. Reese saw the focus of his eyes on her bare hand.

"Because he ain't been able to afford one yet." She explained.

Reese's comment about her fiancé's misfortune amused the overpaid athlete, which was evidenced by the arrogant chuckle that slipped out of his lips. His laughter disgusted Reese, who was fed up with his uppity attitude. She folded her arms and twisted her face to show her displeasure. But Terrance's cocky smile remained as he stared her down. He stood up from his seated position to face her.

"Well, you know what? Since we being so honest about our feelings and sharing secrets, I got something I need to tell you!"

His proclamation sent chills through Reese's body as she automatically began imagining the possibilities of what he was about to say. She waited in silence for his revelation.

"I met this girl, Denise, like two months ago, and we've been dating."

His words were a dagger to Reese's heart. She wanted to hurt him the way his words were hurting her and then find the Denise girl and beat her down. But she knew, with the secret she had just told and the one she had no intention to reveal, she had no place to be angry with him.

"Is that why you didn't want me at your place?"

"Basically." Terrance confirmed. "Denise doesn't live far from me, and I didn't want to risk her stopping by while you were there."

Reese did not like the blunt tone he was using with her. It made her feel as if she was no longer important to him since he found out she was engaged.

"When were you planning on telling me about this?"

"When were you planning on telling me you were engaged?"

His last comment had Reese defeated. She knew nothing she could say would reverse her standing as the villain of the situation. Her stamina for conflict was also wearing thin as the exhaustion of emotion and living for two set in. So she conceded to her worthier adversary.

"So where does this leave *us*?"

Reese knew the answer would probably be unfavorable, but she wanted to know how he was planning to handle their relationship from that point.

"I ain't really down with fucking some other dude's future wifey behind his back. So I'm gonna go back home to be with Denise tonight." Terrance revealed. "And tomorrow, I'll send a car to take you to the airport so you can fly back to your fiancé."

Tears welled in Reese's eyes as she imagined spending her last night in Texas alone.

"So you just gonna leave me here to fend for myself all day."

"They got my credit line downstairs so if you need to order room service, watch a movie, or whatever, be my guest. It's on me."

Terrance tried to hide his pain behind a shallow, insensitive smile.

"Why can't you spend this last night with me and be with her later?"

Reese knew she was trying to light a wet match, but the blaze of her desire for him was still strong.

"Because I'd rather spend my night with someone who actually wants to be with me."

His words extinguished Reese's hopes, and she accepted the fact that her man on the side was ready to move on. Her chest tightened with emotion and left her unable to respond.

Terrance took Reese's silent sniveling as his cue to leave. He forced his right foot to make the first step away from the fiery romance that had him wishing her bare ring finger held the rock he would have no problem affording. But he was tired of competing for her unattainable heart and was ready to try his luck with someone else.

He walked toward the door and grasped the handle upon his arrival in front of it. He looked back into the misty doe eyes of his former lover, giving her one last glimpse into his smoky grey gaze. He pulled the door open and hurled a final farewell.

"Congrats on your engagement."

Chapter 6

January

"Three, two, one. Happy New Year!"

The clock struck 12 midnight, and every person littering the packed dance floor at Club Humidity found the nearest somebody to exchange the first kisses and hugs of the year. As expected, the club's second annual New Year's Eve bash was a great success. The club had reached capacity a little after 11:45, and the line to get in was still winding around the building after the midnight celebration had passed. The party was far from over, and it would be a while before anybody there would get home, especially the frantically busy owner.

Ryan hadn't had a second to himself since the club opened its doors at 9. But he was perfectly fine with all the running around he was doing. It kept his mind off of the fact that the people he cared about most in the world were not present. He wasn't expecting Saniyah to come after their Christmas conflict. The two had only talked at the restaurant when it was absolutely necessary. But he was at least hoping Andre would take a break from playing baby-daddy-does-it-all for Reese and bring in the New Year with him.

He had imagined Saniyah and Andre walking through the door together all night, but he knew after the ball dropped on 2010, that would not be the case. He regretted not being more supportive of his girlfriend's plans, but he was not ready to admit he was wrong. The pride in him was holding off his apology, but the man in him was starving for a woman's touch.

Ryan examined every female face, ass, and chest in the room as he made his way from one chore to the next. Although some parts were nice by themselves, he had yet to find a body with the triple threat to make him forget about the near-perfect woman he was missing.

Just as he was about to give up on his talent search, a Godiva goddess walked up to the bar he was restocking and stole the attention away from his task. He analyzed every inch of her tall, well-built frame from behind the enormous shade of his 6'4" 300-pound bartender, Big Dan.

The black beauty stood about 5'9." Whether the height was all her or she had heels on he couldn't see from his position. What he could see were the pair of perky breasts that hung well without a bra's support underneath the plunging neckline of her bright red, backless halter top.

Further investigation revealed the matching red gauchos clinging for dear life to her rock-hard, round ass that looked to be the product of years in the gym. He tore his eyes away from her curves long enough to find out if the face fit the body. He was presently surprised to find dark brown, ear-length Shirley Temple curls framing almond eyes, high cheek bones, full, glossy lips and an acne-free, wrinkle-free cocoa complexion.

"Let me get a Walk Me Down." She requested in a high-pitched, whiny drawl Ryan had only heard in northern parts of the South. It let him know she wasn't from the area and made him feel more comfortable about approaching. He quickly tapped the bulging shoulder of Big Dan.

"I got this one, D."

Big Dan moved out of the way without another word. He was thankful for the much-needed break from the constant beck and call of drunken strangers and was not about to put up any resistance to his hound-dog boss.

The sexy stranger seemed shocked by the sudden change in staff, but her face warmed into seductive eyes and a cocky, flirtatious smirk when she examined the appearance upgrade of the new bartender. Ryan gave her an enticing smile of his own before turning his attention to making the blue, Sweet 'n Sour concoction she had requested.

"So you one of them fruity drink girls, huh?" Ryan teased to keep her attention.

"Actually, I'm a *woman* who likes her drinks to taste good and hit hard." She corrected.

"Damn. I heard that." Ryan complimented her clever comeback.

So, what's your name, Miss Walk Me Down?" He asked and pushed the alcoholic beverage in front of her.

"Don't you need to be tending to other customers?" She noticed the swell of impatient clubbers piling up behind her.

"Big D got that." Ryan gestured to Big Dan to get back to work. "Besides, I ain't no bartender."

She took a sip of the drink and mocked, "I can tell."

"I see you got jokes."

"Yeah, just a few."

"Well, Miss Joker, what I gotta do to get a name outta you?"

"You can start by telling me why you behind this bar if you ain't no bartender."

"Because when you're the owner, you can be wherever you want."

"You're the owner?" Her eyes light up with surprise and awe. Ryan took notice of her sudden impression with his status and knew his pursuit would be much easier for the remainder of their conversation.

"Yep. Club owner, Ryan Taylor, at your service. And you are…?" He paused in anticipation for her answer.

"Vanessa…Vanessa Spencer."

"Nice to meet you, Miss Vanessa Spencer." Ryan extended his palm, and the pair engaged in an abnormally long first handshake as each one examined the touch of the other.

The new acquaintances made more small talk to further look into each other's background. He told her he was a 26-year-old night club and restaurant owner born and raised in Gulfport, Mississippi. She told him she was a 23-year-old airman stationed at Keesler Air Force Base for the past six months, born and raised in Columbus, Georgia. But their conversation was cut short when Vanessa's favorite song "Get Loose" by T.I. blasted from the speakers, prompting her to drag Ryan to the dance floor.

Vanessa winded on him so well in the crowded space that he began to imagine what she would do to him behind closed doors. His lust for her grew and was apparent underneath his khaki slacks.

"I got you excited down there. Don't I, Mr. Taylor?" She turned to face him and show her amusement with his body language.

"Yeah. What you planning on doing about that, Miss Spencer?" Ryan didn't know what kind of reaction to expect from the woman he barely knew, but he gave her an intense stare to let her know he was serious.

"You got somewhere we can be alone?" She whispered into his ear.

Without answering her question, Ryan grabbed her hand and guided her through the maze of bouncing bodies and up the stairs to his second floor office. Normally, he would have taken her directly to his apartment, but it reeked of Saniyah. Her clothes were in his closet and the pictures they took together were on display. Even his sheets and pillow cases still held the scent of her perfume, which he knew because he hadn't washed them just to feel closer to her.

Ryan unlocked the office door and relocked it once they were both securely inside. Before he had a chance to say another word, Vanessa leaned into him and smothered his lips. Her hands went immediately to the work of unbuckling and unzipping his pants. Both tasks were done within seconds, and his loose-fitting pants fell to the floor without assistance.

Vanessa guided her lover for the evening behind his desk and pushed him down into his computer chair. She fell to her knees and had him out of his boxers and in her mouth faster than any other woman he had ever been with. The sensation made him numb and he fell back in the chair with closed eyes. Once the feeling in his body returned, he ran his fingers through her tight curls and palmed the back of her head to guide the experience.

When he felt she had control of the situation, he removed his grasp and returned to his numb state of pure ecstasy. He went so far into his numbness that he forgot who he was with. So when his toes started curling and his eyes started rolling back, he called out the first name that came to mind.

"Damn, Niyah! You killing me, Girl." He moaned.

"Who the fuck is *Niyah*?"

Ryan's rolling eyes bucked out of his head and brought him back into reality. He stared down into the angry face that was so far from Saniyah's he couldn't imagine how he had confused the two. The look in her red-hot eyes let him know their sexual encounter was over and demanded an explanation at the same time. He saw no reward in lying so he gave her an honest response.

"She's my ex. We just broke up."

At his words, Vanessa lifted from her kneeling position and made her way to the door. She was going to leave without another word, but when she looked back at his defeated frame slumping in the chair, she was inspired to speak before making her exit.

"I ain't no rebound hoe. So when you finally get over this Niyah chick, holler at me."

Chapter 7

Ryan awoke to the sweet smell of Saniyah's favorite scent, still lingering in the fabric of his bed clothes. Before lifting his head from the pillow she used to sleep on, he took in a long inhalation of the enchanting fragrance. The memory of his awkward sexual encounter with Vanessa was still fresh in his mind and had brought a lot of things into perspective for him. Most important was the fact that even when he was with another, equally gorgeous, obviously different woman, he couldn't keep his mind off of Saniyah.

As he lifted up from his bed and made his way into the bathroom, he thought.

"I gotta get back with my baby."

Right then, he made it his New Year's Day mission to do whatever he had to do to patch up his relationship. He took down mental notes about what it was going to take to make that happen while going through his preparation for the day.

By the time he was dressed and ready to walk out of the door, he knew exactly how to get his lady back home. There would be a few stops along the way, but the ultimate goal of his journey would be to get through Reese's front door and back into Saniyah's arms.

Reese sat at the kitchen table watching Saniyah slave over the pots and pans that would eventually hold their New Year's Day dinner. The entire apartment was filled with the smells of honey-cured ham, black-eyed peas, candied yams, collard greens, macaroni and cheese casserole and cornbread. Reese's two stomachs were yearning for the satisfaction the food was sure to bring. So as a disguise to her anticipation of receiving the first taste, she exploited her cousin's craving for conversation as she cooked.

The two were in the middle of a chat about the attractive, single new neighbor that had just moved into the building across from them when the doorbell rang throughout the apartment. Reese went to answer the door expecting to see her and Saniyah's parents -- who were all en route to her apartment for dinner. When she saw Ryan instead, standing in her doorway with a fresh bouquet of yellow roses, her smile melted into a twisted scowl.

"If you looking for Andre, he ain't here. He's driving up to Jackson to see his daddy." She snapped.

"Why would I come to see a dude with flowers?" He smirked at the absurdity of her comment.

"I don't know. Is it something you need to tell me about your relationship with my man?" Reese knew her comment would sting any straight man's ego in the homophobic South, and that was her intention.

"Ha, ha, ha. Girl, you know who I came here for."

"*Correction.* I know who you didn't come here for 'cause she *don't* wanna see you." Reese informed.

Ryan did not know the amount of truth in Reese's comment, but he was expecting her to be a barrier whether Saniyah wanted to see him or not. He pulled a king-sized box of Lemon Heads out of the inside pocket of his navy blue pea coat. Reese's hungry eyes were immediately drawn to the sound of the hard candies crashing into one another as they fell from one end of the box to the other. Her attention let Ryan know she was interested, and he said a silent prayer of thanks for remembering when Andre mentioned they were her favorite candy.

"What's that for?" Reese said through watering lips.

"A peace offering."

Ryan's eyes pleaded with Reese for understanding.

"You really think I'm gonna let you worm your way back into my cousin's life for some candy?"

Reese stood with an unimpressed pout and both hands on her hips.

"Oh. So you don't want them?" Ryan said as he began to put the big yellow box back into his coat pocket, but Reese grabbed his hand.

"I didn't say all that." Reese said before snatching the sweets out of his hands. "Just don't tell Niyah I sold her out for Lemon Heads."

Reese pushed her body against the door, moving it back to the wall to allow him entry.

"She's in the kitchen." Reese directed with her pointing index finger and outstretched arm, the other clutching the candy box against her chest.

"Thanks." Ryan said before sealing his exit to the kitchen with a swift kiss to Reese's cheek that she immediately wiped off in disgust.

Ryan entered the kitchen holding the roses over his heart and was greeted by Saniyah's gorgeous figure in a pink fitted wife beater and tight dark blue skinny jeans. Her back was turned as she hovered over the stove. Her full focus was on stirring and seasoning.

"Smells good, Boo." Ryan spoke sweetly.

His words brought Saniyah out of her food-filled trance. She released her metal stirring spoon into the syrupy soup surrounding her yams and turned to face Ryan.

"What you want?"

"I came to apologize." Ryan explained and walked over to her, extending the flowers upon his arrival. "And to give you these."

Saniyah took the flowers but showed no emotion about receiving them.

"You don't like them?"

"The flowers are fine, Ryan, but why did it take you so long to give them to me?"

Ryan felt the ache in her words and realized the task before him was not going to play out as easily as he had imagined in his bathroom that morning.

"I'm sorry, Boo." He pleaded. "My pride wouldn't let me admit I was wrong."

"Well, are you admitting it now?"

Ryan sought the strength to push the painful admission out of his mouth and was motivated by the look on Saniyah's face letting him know that was what it would take to win her over.

"Yes. I was wrong, and I'm truly sorry." He confirmed and put his right hand over his heart to illustrate his sincerity. He grasped her free hand with his left.

"Does that mean you'll support my restaurant dream?"

"With all my heart..." Ryan promised. "...As long as you continue to support mine."

Saniyah looked away from his stare to think about what he proposed. She had not put much thought into the obligations she would face playing dual roles as the chef of two restaurants -- one of which she would also have to help build from the ground up. But she was not willing to give him the upper hand in their disagreement by refusing his attempt to compromise.

"I think I can handle that."

Saniyah's willingness to accept his terms showed in her softening eyes and slight smile. Ryan pulled her into his arms, crushing the flowers she held between their bodies. The reconciled couple shared a passionate kiss to seal their agreement and then held their embrace to become reacquainted with each other's touch.

"You staying for dinner?" Saniyah uttered a sweet invitation.

Ryan took in the intoxicating aroma of her New Year's feast before giving his response.

"As long as I get served by my Baby."

Chapter 8

Andre pulled into the parking lot of the Boiling Point after two days of groveling at the feet of his strong-willed father. For the first time since filling up at a Richland gas station that morning, his car came to a halt in front of the calm waters and afternoon horizon on the Mississippi Sound.

His attempt to make a speedy exit from the vehicle was impeded by the sudden tug of the seatbelt he had forgotten to unbuckle. He quickly released himself from the restraint and practically skipped to the front entrance of the soul food establishment. He paused before entering, partly to calm his excitement for the announcement he had to make and partly because he had forgotten to initiate the alarm on his Mustang.

He waited for the beep and flashing headlights that signaled his car's protection and then made his way inside to the smiling hostess waiting to greet him at her podium.

"Hello, Sir. Table for one?" She assumed reaching to the side of the podium to grab a single menu. The acne on her adolescent face showed clearly through the pound of brown foundation she had piled on to disguise it. The face craters had Andre mesmerized, and his blank, analyzing stare agitated her tone in her second effort to seat him.

"Sir, is it just one in your party?" Her new, slightly unprofessional tone snapped Andre out of his daze.

"Actually, I'm here to see the chef. I'm her friend, Andre. Can you tell her I need to speak with her?"

Without another word, she dropped the menu back into the side compartment, picked up the podium phone and dialed three digits. Her stance relaxed when she heard the familiarity in the voice that picked up on the other end.

"Hey, somebody out here needs to speak with Miss Saniyah…Says his name's Andre." All professionalism had left her tone and let Andre know his identification as a non-paying, non-customer made him no longer relevant.

After a slight pause, the hostess gave Andre instructions.

"She said to have a seat at the bar, and she'll be right with you."

"Thanks." Andre gave a smile that was returned by an uncaring glare.

"No problem."

He made his way to the unoccupied bar and had a seat on the stool right in the middle. The only people around were the bartender and a waitress filling a soda order at the nearby beverage station.

"Hey, can I get Hennessey on the rocks?" He yelled to the bartender who was wiping down the far end of the bar. The bartender nodded to acknowledge Andre's request and walked over to retrieve the cognac from the clutter of liquor bottles lining the shelves on the bar's back wall. He sat the drink in front of Andre just as Saniyah walked up to greet him.

"Hey, Dre. What's up?" She smiled through the pain of being on her feet for the past few hours. Andre couldn't help noticing how attractive she remained even though her French-braided hair was disheveled, her face was bare, and her white chef coat was stained with brown gravy.

His face lit up as the excitement he had suppressed until that point rebuilt itself inside him. He took both of her hands in his and looked her straight in the eye. The fanatical smile on his face revealed the immensity of his announcement.

"My dad agreed to do it!" The octave in his tone rose to a giddy gasp. It took a moment for Saniyah to process the meaning in his declaration. But her understanding soon showed in her wide, dancing eyes and ear-to-ear smile.

"Shut up!"

"I'm serious."

"But how?"

"I convinced him that it was a good investment."

"Excuse me, Sir. That drink will be seven dollars." Up until that point, the bartender had patiently waited with bill in hand. But when he realized the depth of the conversation, he knew he would have to interrupt in order to collect.

Andre slipped the bartender one of the twenties in the hundred dollars his father had forced into his pocket that morning. He took the first sip from his drink while waiting for the bartender to return his change, but Saniyah could not wait for his return before reigniting the conversation.

"So how did you do it?" She blurted as the bartender slapped thirteen dollars down in front of Andre. He returned eleven of them to his wallet and immediately went into his explanation of how he used his business know-how to win his father over.

Andre explained that he was prepared for success as soon as he knocked on his father's door clutching two containers filled with the fried catfish, potato casserole, buttermilk biscuits and bread pudding with wine sauce Saniyah cooked the night before he left for Jackson. His father promptly devoured the food and was convinced of Saniyah's undeniable talent.

Once his father's belly was full, Andre presented him with a business proposal for Saniyah's restaurant, including how profits would reimburse the use of his resources and his financial investment. His father was intrigued by the plan but not totally on board so Andre took it a step further and explained how his tight-fisted patriarch could cruise his connections for other investors to lighten the financial burden.

But his father was still not ready to commit to the project without more thought; that Andre knew would result in rejection. So Andre pulled out the big guns of emotional appeal and guilt-tripped his father about not supporting the career ambitions that would give his *only* son the ability to provide

for his *only* grandchild. The meeting resulted in a

tear-stained apology from Andre's father seeking

forgiveness for not spending more time with him

when he was young followed by his confirmation

that he would do whatever Andre needed to make

the restaurant a success.

"So you had to put the guilt trip on him,

huh?" Saniyah brought Andre out of his

enterprising trance.

"Yeah. I knew he still felt kind of bad about

what happened with Mama."

"Did they have a bad divorce or

something?" Saniyah did not mean to pry, but his

revelation had intrigued her.

"No. She died when I was ten, and my dad

turned all his focus to work to keep his mind off of

it." Andre usually did not like pouring out his

painful past, but he felt surprisingly comfortable sharing it with Saniyah.

"I'm sorry, Dre. I didn't know."

"It was a long time ago. I'm cool with it." Andre lied. Not a day had gone by without him having some memory, fond or sorrowful, of his short time with his loving mother. And lately, many nights had ended with him crying on Reese's pregnant belly thinking about how his mother would not be a part of their child's life.

"If you don't mind me asking, how did she die?" Saniyah reluctantly continued her dive into Andre's personal life.

"She had breast cancer."

His words sent chills up Saniyah's spine as her mind filled with memories of the grandmother she was still grieving.

"Really? I lost my grandmother to breast cancer a few years back."

An unexpected rush of emotion sent tears streaming down Saniyah's cheeks, and she tried, unsuccessfully, to hold in her sorrowful shriek. Andre lifted from his bar stool and embraced his weeping friend. Her tears melted into the fabric of his grey hoodie as her face brushed against his chest. Both felt comforted and bonded by the similarity in their backgrounds and the closeness of their touch that was brewing compassion with every second it lasted.

"I guess I didn't realize how much I still miss her?"

Saniyah pulled away from his embrace and covered her face with both hands, slightly embarrassed by her display of weakness and her attraction to the feel of her cousin's fiancé.

"It's okay to miss her…You should miss her. I still miss my mom, too, but I know she's watching over me just like your grandma is watching over you."

The warmth of his words and the massage of his hand on her shoulder soothed her heartache and further stirred her forbidden desires.

"And you know both of them are gonna have our backs in this restaurant thing." Andre continued to comfort her. His comment reminded her of the celebration her emotional outburst was dampening.

"So how soon you think your dad can have it up and running?" She choked on her words as she tried to relax the tightness in her throat.

"If we can find a place by March, he'll have the doors open by June."

Chapter 9

June

Just as Andre had predicted five months before, the doors to Southern Sizzle were ready to open right on schedule. All preparation was complete and the June 15 grand opening had finally arrived.

From the beginning stages, Saniyah's restaurant dream seemed destined to come to fruition. Andre's father had provided all construction and interior design services free of charge. His real estate guru best friend had also located the perfect piece of property on the land side of Casino Row on Highway 90 in Biloxi -- which he also purchased as his own investment in the business venture. And to Saniyah's surprise, her parents had also chipped in on the cost of supplies to show their support.

Everything had come together so quickly and so perfectly that Saniyah could hardly believe it was not a dream that she was standing in the middle of her own restaurant counting down the minutes to its 7 p.m. premiere. She looked around and imagined the great first impression guests would have after experiencing the unique dining experience her establishment would provide.

Upon their arrival, guests would be greeted by an atmosphere that she and Andre had spent countless hours ensuring could be experienced nowhere else on the Coast. The menu was her signature blend of upscale cuisine and traditional southern soul and seafood favorites, with the marquee dishes being filet mignon and fried grits and a lobster gumbo served over creamy potato salad. The bar was stocked with only the finest top-shelf liquor and champagne. And due to Andre's father's own contribution to the design, the restaurant stood over a state-of-the art underground wine cellar custom built to ensure quality taste in every bottle.

Aside from pleasing the stomach, the restaurant would also please the spirit. Some of the best jazz and blues acts from around the state of Mississippi were scheduled to perform for months in advance. Every guest would be seated and served with class by a staff that had undergone a grueling three-month training regimen to learn proper serving etiquette and techniques. And Saniyah's kitchen team was composed of her former classmates who were familiar with her style so that no taste would be lost in her absence.

Saniyah and Andre were the first ones to arrive and were making some final adjustments before the big reveal. After one last checklist run through, they decided the place was as ready as it was going to be and wanted to share an opening-night toast before their staff and guests arrived. Saniyah sat at the bar while Andre went behind it to prepare two glasses of champagne. He handed one to her and leaned across the bar to make his toast.

"Here's to…Southern Sizzle and its creators. May this newfound partnership be successful."

Andre said a silent prayer hoping the words in his toast would reach God's ear. The pair touched glasses, and the clink of the fluted shapes resonated throughout the empty atmosphere. The two raised their glasses to their lips and the sting of the bubbly beverage in their throats gave them both a bitter grimace.

"Can you believe this day is here already?" Saniyah squeaked.

"I know. It seems like, just yesterday, we were still planning this stuff in the living room."

Andre admired the elegant eatery and reminisced on their journey from ground breaking to grand opening.

"Well, Andre, I just want to take this opportunity to thank you 'cause I couldn't have done any of this without you."

Saniyah sat her glass down on the bar and clutched Andre's hand. She stared up into his statuesque face and was mesmerized by the happy glimmer in his eyes.

"You don't have to thank me. If it wasn't for you, I'd probably be trying to figure out how to raise a kid on the street right now."

Andre noticed her fixed eyes upon him and felt compelled, with a little help from the bubbling bravery he was sipping, to make a confession.

"Niyah, you ever had feelings for somebody you weren't supposed to?"

"I think I do right now."

Saniyah made her own unexpected confession. Her drunken lips were speaking sober thoughts; thoughts she had no intention of ever revealing to her *cousin's* fiancé. The pair held an immersed gaze upon each other not noticing how their bodies were narrowing the gap between them. Andre gently grasped Saniyah's chin. She closed her eyes to spare them of what would come next. He pulled her lips into his and breathed in the chocolate smell of her lip gloss as their mouths touched. But their forbidden kiss was cut short by a loud, banging knock on the locked front entrance.

Andre's eyes bulged out of his head as he pulled his lips away from Saniyah's kiss. He scrambled from behind the bar to open the door praying Reese was not on the other side. He wiped his lips and took a breath before revealing the intruder, who turned out to be a kitchen staff worker coming in early. Andre showed the eager employee to the kitchen and then returned to the uncomfortable silence of the dining room.

After a few more speechless moments of the pair stealing ashamed glimpses of one another, Andre decided to break the silence. He walked over to Saniyah and sat on the bar stool on side of her.

"I'm sorry, Saniyah. I was *so* out of line for doing that."

"Well, it wasn't like I tried to stop you."

Both of them stared straight ahead at the wall separating the bar from the kitchen.

"You not gonna tell Reese, are you?" Andre pleaded.

"Hell no! Are you gonna tell Ryan?"

"Hell, hell, hell no!"

The two shared an anxious laugh.

"Look, let's just forget this happened and enjoy tonight. We'll have plenty of time to figure out what that was later." Saniyah reasoned.

"Yeah." Andre agreed. "We got a restaurant to open."

Ryan staggered up the steps of a Bayou View apartment building and leaned his intoxicated body against the door to apartment 205 before placing a slight tap against its cold, metal frame. When he realized his tap was not strong enough to alert the owner of his presence, he began banging his fist into the door. It suddenly jerked open, and he almost fell into the apartment before grabbing the door frame to catch his balance. He looked up into the almond eyes of his military mistress.

"Damn, Nigga. Why you banging on my door like you the police?"

Vanessa's slightly annoyed expression soon softened with compassion at the sight of her disoriented caller.

"You okay, Boo?" She purred.

"I'm good, Girl." Ryan confirmed. "Just full of that Yac."

His attempt to hide the extent of his intoxication was unsuccessful as every word he spoke slurred out of his mouth.

"Yeah, you good alright...good and drunk." Vanessa laughed as she helped him into her apartment. She nearly had to drag him to the couch, and they both fell on top of the soft, suede cushions.

Once she had regained her posture, she pulled him upright and lifted his feet to rest on the coffee table in front of them.

"You sure know how to take care of your man. Don't you?" Ryan spoke through heavy lips and nearly lost control of his even heavier eyelids.

"So, you my man now?"

Vanessa did not know whether to feel uncomfortable about his drunken statement of commitment, but she decided to play along.

"If you want me to be?"

"Don't you think your girl gonna have a problem with that?"

In their numerous phone conversations after meeting, Ryan had made it very clear to Vanessa that he was back with his girlfriend and had no intentions of leaving her.

"Man, fuck her. In fact, don't even mention her to me no more."

Ryan cringed at the thought of his relationship. It had been on thin ice since he and Saniyah made up on New Year's, and the resolve she had to ignore him while getting her restaurant up and running had not made it any less fragile. Her preoccupancy was driving a wedge between them, and Ryan was losing interest in their disconnected relationship.

"Damn. What did she do to you?"

"She's been so wrapped up in her own thing lately. I don't think she even knows she got a man anymore."

Vanessa could feel the hurt in his admission.

"Aww, poor baby. You want Nessa to make you feel better?" She caressed his face and pulled his head into her lap.

"I ain't gonna fight you if you try."

"I think I got just the thing to put you in a better mood, Boo."

Vanessa bent down and kissed his cheek before sliding out from under him to make her way into the kitchen. Ryan slumped down onto the couch. His drowsy eyes watched the sway of her chocolate curves as she moved further from his view.

When she returned, she held two cocktail glasses filled with an unidentifiable white liquid. He sat up from his drunken slump to receive the glass he assumed was filled with liquor.

"You trying to get me drunk, Miss Spencer?"

His drooping face lifted into a sly smile.

"You already took care of that yourself. This is water. Maybe it'll help you sober up some."

Ryan was a bit disappointed by it, but he accepted the life-giving beverage and took a few sips to cool the cognac burn in his belly. Vanessa sat beside him and sipped from her own glass. He noticed bubbles rising and heard a fizzing sound as the drink rushed back into the bottom of her glass.

"That's not water you sipping on."

"I know. It's Sprite and Absolut."

"Well, where is this remedy you got to make me feel better? I know it ain't just this water."

Although the water was calming his high, Ryan was in need of sexual healing, and the sight of Vanessa's soft lips taking sips from her glass was raising his temperature.

"Hold on, Baby. Let me finish my drink and get closer to your level."

"You gonna make me wait for it?"

"Good things are worth waiting for, Mr. Taylor."

She gave him a teasing glance before taking another sip of her drink.

"Now, tell me more about the problems you having with your girl?"

She sat back with folded legs and scrutinizing eyes ready to analyze his every word with a psychiatrist's precision. Ryan gladly filled her in on his relationship woes. He told her how Saniyah's restaurant dream had put their relationship on the back burner and that he was starting to feel neglected. He told her about the grand opening celebration he was missing to be with her because he couldn't bear to be a part of what was killing his love life. And finally, he told her that he felt like he was falling out of love with

Saniyah and sometimes could not even stand to be around her during the few times they were together.

"That's some cold shit." Vanessa commented, blown away by the depth of the information he was sharing. And his need for affection had her mind working on a plan to supply it.

"I know."

"If you feel that way, why don't you just leave her?"

"That...I don't know." Ryan admitted.

Vanessa saw the wearied look on his face and knew her question had troubled his mind.

"Well, don't worry, Boo. Nessa knows just how to ease your stress."

Her words revved Ryan's engine and made his thoughts move from depression to seduction.

"How?"

"We need to get wet!"

"*Get wet*?" Ryan blurted. "If that's your way of saying we need to get high, I ain't down with that, Ma."

"No, fool." She laughed. "There's a pool downstairs. You wanna take a dip?"

"Oh shit!" Ryan laughed at his off-base assumption. "We skinny dipping?"

"If you're lucky."

Vanessa exited to her room, and Ryan anxiously awaited her return. When she came back into the living room, her nudity was barely hidden underneath the skimpy, red string bikini she was sporting.

"You do like that red. Don't you?" Ryan remembered the outfit that had attracted his attention on New Year's.

"It's my favorite color."

"It looks damn good on you, too."

He examined every bit of her mocha frame exposed by the scarcity of her bathing suit. Her arms and legs were perfectly toned. Her breasts sat on her chest like two scoops of double fudge ice cream. And her stomach was accented by the indention of a subtle six pack that was still feminine and sexy.

"So you ready to go?" Vanessa asked.

Ryan practically ripped the clothes from his body until he stood in nothing but his eight-ball boxer shorts.

"I'm ready now."

"I can see that." Vanessa smiled as she took a glimpse at the bulge growing in his boxers.

When they got to the outdoor pool, Ryan wasted no time. He leaped into it, causing an eruption of water to reach for the sky. The unexpected freeze sent chills through his body.

"Got damn, this water is cold!" His lips started to quiver and he wrapped himself in his arms in an effort to generate some unlikely body heat.

Vanessa strolled to the ladder in the middle of the pool and slowly lowered her body into the brisk water. The midsection was only five feet deep, so her feet reached comfortably to the bottom of the pool. Ryan swam over to her from the deep end. His stroke splashed water in every direction.

"Chill with all that. I ain't trying to get my hair wet." Ryan noticed her curls were pinned to the top of her head with a big black hair clip.

"You might as well say goodbye to that perm, Boo. 'Cause when I get through, you gonna need another one." Ryan pressed his body into hers as he wrapped her lips into a watery kiss. She stumbled backwards until she found structure against the pool wall.

Vanessa wrapped her legs around his waist and moved her lips down to his neck and upper chest. Her take-charge attitude turned him on, and his bulge was begging for release. He pulled out of his boxers, and his buoy bobbed in the water as his hand went in search of Vanessa's bikini bottom. He snatched it down as far as it would go and penetrated the cold chlorine depths until he reached Vanessa's warm waters.

She cried out into the dark, humid night as he entered her body. She wrapped her arms around his shoulders and dug her acrylic nails into the crevices of his back. The sting of her clutches excited Ryan. He pumped harder into her causing her body to slam violently into the pool wall. The pain in her back did not compare to the pleasure between her legs so she drowned it out.

Water rippled vigorously off of their bodies as Ryan increased the velocity of his stroke. But he soon calmed it to a pause when he heard the slam of a car door and footsteps approaching. He put his index finger over Vanessa's mouth to silence her moans until the footsteps went away. She found this to be a troubling task to accomplish with his buoy still floating in her waters, but she mustered the strength to suppress her sex shrieks until the footsteps were no longer audible.

Ryan rekindled his stroke with the same ferocity. This time it was so damaging, Vanessa could not ignore the painful slams her body was enduring.

"Slow down. You gonna break my back."

Her voice trembled with every hit against the cement. But her plea for mercy went unacknowledged as Ryan continued his pummeling until he felt the pressure of orgasm building inside him. He pulled away from her body just in time for his baby brew to shoot down to the bottom of the pool. He rested his exhausted body on top of her banged up frame and she dropped her forehead into his shoulder.

"So…" Vanessa breathed out. "You feel better now?"

Ryan walked through the door to his apartment around 3 a.m. and was greeted by the blurred vision of Saniyah's scolding face. She was seated in the recliner wearing her comfortable silk night gown, but her posture was far from relaxed. Not wanting to deal with whatever she had to dish out, he walked a straight path to his bedroom door.

But as expected, Saniyah's voice halted his stride.

"Do you know what time it is?" She

scolded him with a surprisingly calm disposition

and tone.

"I got a watch."

His snide remark came from behind as he

was still facing the direction of his bedroom.

"Well, where the Hell have you been?"

"I had to fill in for Big D at the club

tonight."

"Don't lie to me."

"How you figure I'm lying?"

He turned to face her accusation.

"'Cause I just called the club an hour ago,

and *Big D* told me you hadn't been there."

"Oh, so now you checking up on me?"

"What you expect me to do when you come home at four in the morning and you not answering your phone?"

Her calm tone was quickly building into a tempered bark. Ryan pulled his Blackberry from his pocket and saw the ten missed calls he assumed all came from Saniyah. He fidgeted with the phone before shoving it back in his pocket stalling for time to put together a response.

"Well, if you really wanna know…me and my boy, Slim, went to get a daiquiri from Orangutang's and shot pool."

Saniyah knew his words were false before they fully left his lips. Not only had she never heard him mention "Slim" before, but she also knew Ryan did not like to spend money in other bars when he could drink free at his own. Her anger melted into hurt at his inconsiderate and blatantly dishonest excuse, and her eyes glazed over with tears.

"So that was more important than my grand opening?" She choked on her words.

"Oh, that was tonight?" Ryan added fuel to the flames with his nonchalant attitude.

"You know, damn well, it was tonight! Don't give me that shit!" Saniyah screamed through the pain of her tightening throat.

"Whatever. You probably didn't want me there anyway." Ryan raised his voice.

"Why would you say that? Of course I wanted you there." Saniyah lowered her tone.

"Well, you ain't been acting like you wanted me around lately?"

Saniyah realized that his bad behavior was a reaction to her neglect. She could not recall the last time the two of them had shared an entire hour together, and sex had been nonexistent ever since she started working on her restaurant. With all the responsibilities she was juggling to build Southern Sizzle, she hadn't even been able to keep her promise to him to continue cooking at the Boiling Point.

Saniyah walked over to Ryan and grabbed both of his hands. Her apologetic eyes and pleading pout warmed his heart.

"I'm sorry, Baby. I didn't realize how much you been missing me. Can you forgive me if I promise to spend more time with you?"

"You know I can't say no to that face." He smiled. "And I'm sorry about missing your big night. How was it?"

Saniyah's mind filled with the events of the gratifyingly smooth opening night she had just experienced and her face lit up with excitement.

"It was wonderful…." She paused abruptly. Her rave was cut short by the smell of lavender permeating the air from Ryan's direction.

"Why do you smell like that?"

"Smell like what?"

"Like you're wearing a woman's perfume."

Ryan's mind flashed back to sitting in Vanessa's room watching her dress after their pool rendezvous and how she had playfully sprayed her perfume bottle at him. He knew he was caught, but he was not about to admit his wrongdoing.

"What you think I'm cheating on you now?" Ryan freed his hands from her grasp to illustrate his frustration with all of her nagging accusations. But his incriminating response and uncomfortable posture filled Saniyah in on what had really kept him away from her opening night.

"I didn't say I did. But are you?"

"No. I'm not cheating on you." He grunted. "Happy?"

"No."

"Oh, well, I don't know what to tell you then."

Ryan shrugged his shoulders and turned away from her to make an exit to his room before he revealed anymore evidence of his infidelity. But Saniyah gripped his shoulder to impede his escape.

"Where you think you going? This ain't over!" She commanded.

Her dominant tone and firm hold enraged Ryan. He shifted around and put all the momentum of his turn into a brutal slap to her cheek that sent her body crashing down to the floor. He looked down at her broken, sobbing frame with a menacing glare. She shielded herself with her arms trying to avoid a second blow.

"Bitch, don't you ever put your hands on me like that again!" He shouted. "Trying to tell me what to do...you think you run this or something?"

"No, Baby. I'm sorry." Saniyah pleaded.

"Damn right, you sorry. 'Cause I run this. I'm the man in this relationship." He smashed his index finger into his chest unintentionally imitating the pound of King Kong.

"You're right. You're the man." Saniyah agreed to calm the situation.

"And don't ever forget that."

Ryan was pleased by her frail, defeated disposition so he began to walk back to his bedroom entertained by her symphony of sobs. But before he was out of sight, he left her with words to illustrate his displeasure with her behavior.

"I suggest you make your bed out here tonight."

Chapter 10

"Here's your daughter, Miss Dixon." A nurse said before carefully maneuvering the 7 lb.-11 ounce swaddled bundle of joy out of her experienced cuddle and into Reese's trembling arms.

This baby was the first Reese had ever held, and from the moment the child was placed in her arms, she was paralyzed by the fear of doing it wrong. She looked down at the calm face of the miniature sleeping beauty and tried to grasp that this baby was, in fact, *her child*. The realization set in that she was responsible for the well-being of a life other than her own. Uncertainty swelled up inside her. She thought.

"Am I really ready for this?"

She pulled her daughter's tiny, wrinkled hand out of her mouth. The child wrapped her fingers around her mother's pinky. Reese smiled as their bodies reconnected for the first time since she gave birth. And the love she had been building for that little girl since she felt the first kick overturned all her fears.

"Damn, Reese, she is beautiful!"

Andre was already smitten with the little lady he had only met two hours ago. He sat beside Reese on the hospital bed and wrapped his fiancée and daughter in his protective embrace. He leaned in and placed a soft kiss on his little one's forehead. Then he smiled at Reese and caressed her chin before pulling her face into their first kiss as parents.

"Well, at least one of us is beautiful up in here."

Reese fondled her disheveled, uncombed hair while shedding invisible tears over the depressed state of her formerly flawless figure.

"I know." Andre laughed as he examined the plaid drawstring pajama pants and bleach-stained black wife beater he was wearing. Reese's water broke at two a.m. leaving neither of them time to do much more than grab her hospital bag and jump in the car.

"Ya'll two pretty motherfuckers need to shut up." Reese's mom, Angela, barked as she emerged from the bathroom. She had driven in from Mobile to be at Reese's side during the delivery and had been twisting Reese's patience the entire time with her crude commentary and insufficient affection.

"Mama, don't talk like that in front of Adriana!"

"Aww Hell…you act like the girl gonna know what I'm talking about one day out the squat."

"Damn, do you have to be so vulgar all the time? You're a grandmother now. Act like one!" Reese sneered at her outspoken mother.

"Yeah, I'm a grandmother, but you better remember I'm still your mama!" Angela snuffed her daughter's attempt to scold her behavior. She knew her actions were getting under her daughter's skin. With all the drama Reese had caused in her teen years, Angela had developed a guilty pleasure in making her only child squirm as an adult. And Reese's spitting-image resemblance and identical whorish ways to Angela's "low down" ex-husband did little to help the strained mother-daughter relationship.

"Mama, look…" Reese sat up and started to object, but Andre cut her off. He saw the smirk on Angela's face and the vein popping out of Reese's neck and knew a family faceoff would ensue unless he distracted them from the tension.

"Hey, Ang, we haven't eaten all day. You mind going to Taco Bell to get us something to eat?" His eyes pleaded with his mother-in-law-to-be to stop irritating his exhausted fiancée and fulfill his request.

"Alright, I guess I can do that." Angela smacked. "What ya'll want?"

Reese relaxed at her mother's conceding words and leaned back onto the bed. The couple placed their order, and Angela grabbed her purse to make the run.

"Well, let me kiss my grandbaby good bye before I go." Angela said before walking up to her daughter's side. Their argument still had Reese on edge, and she was almost reluctant to allow her mother's filth-spewing lips to touch her daughter's soft, sensitive cheek. But she allowed her mother to kiss the resting infant. Angela then made her way to the door and was about to walk out when Saniyah walked through the door.

"Hey, Girl!" Angela announced Saniyah's arrival before pulling her niece into a quick embrace.

"Hi, Auntie."

Angela examined Saniyah's thin frame and admired the cute floral sun dress she was wearing.

"That dress is beautiful, and you look gorgeous in it."

Reese rolled her eyes. It blew her mind that she had just given birth to a beautiful little girl, and the first positive thing out of her mother's mouth was about her cousin's dress.

"Thank you." Saniyah blushed from the attention.

"Well, I'm gone to get these two knuckleheads something to eat so I'll see you later on." Angela waved and then vanished from sight down the hall toward the elevator.

"Hey, *Mom*!" Saniyah smiled as she made her way over to give her cousin a congratulatory hug.

"Congratulations!" She looked from Reese to Andre. She hurried to rip her eyes from Andre's enticing face, and he awkwardly did the same. Memories of their opening night kiss were still fresh in both of their minds, and neither of them wanted to give Reese any indication that something was going on between them.

Saniyah's wondering eyes landed in Reese's arms as she took in her first up-close glimpse of the newest addition to their family.

"She is precious. You know you gotta let me hold her...since it was my cooking' that ran her out the belly." Saniyah laughed.

Reese had been having false alarms and contractions in the days following Southern Sizzle's opening night and went into labor the following week after eating there again the night before.

Reese carefully handed her baby over to her cousin's excited embrace. Saniyah walked the baby over to the purse she had sat down on the couch. She retrieved it and then tossed it onto the bed beside Reese.

"Look in there. I brought you something." Saniyah instructed without taking her eyes off of the infant in her arms.

"Aww…Lemon Heads! Thank you, Girl!" Reese's eyes lit up as she hurried to open the box and pop one of the tangy candies into her mouth.

"No problem, Girl. You know I got you."

"So where's Ryan?" Reese tore her attention away from the sugar serenading her mouth to realize he was missing in action.

"I don't know, and I could care less." Saniyah's words were firm even as she was making silly faces at Adriana.

"What, you two fighting again?" Reese was becoming frustrated with her cousin's on-again, off-again romance.

"He's still tripping over this restaurant thing." The sting in her still aching face kept her lips tight about the abuse.

"Well, you want Andre to talk to him about it?"

"Yeah, that's a good idea." Andre agreed. "I might be able to get him to loosen up."

Saniyah appreciated the offer, but she knew it would only lead to more violent attacks from Ryan for spreading their business.

"Thanks for the offer, but I think this is something we need to settle between ourselves." Saniyah was in no mood to discuss the stresses of her relationship and suddenly had the urge to leave before Andre and her snooping cousin started to pry their noses into it. She handed Adriana back to Reese and retrieved her purse.

"I gotta go." Saniyah leaned in to kiss Reese and then turned to hug Andre before heading toward the door. Reese noticed her sour expression and her sudden urgency to leave and knew something was wrong.

"Niyah, is everything okay?" Reese's words halted her cousin's exit. Saniyah turned around to face her cousin's worried eyes and formed a lie to ease her mind.

"Yeah, Girl. I just remembered I got a shipment of steaks coming in today, and I want to be there to make sure it's what I ordered."

Andre heard her words and knew it was a lie immediately. She had already told him the meat order was not coming in until two days later. He didn't understand why she would use a lie she knew he knew was false. But he did understand what she was trying to cover with her dishonesty.

"Okay…just checking. Bye, girl." Reese called as her cousin walked out of the room. When Saniyah was gone, Reese turned to face Andre still wearing the worried look.

"Baby, you think something's wrong with her?" Andre knew exactly what was wrong with Saniyah, but he was not about to excite his fresh-out-of-delivery fiancée with the revelation. He knew it was not his place to discuss his hunch, especially without anything to back it up. And he felt it was something Saniyah would have to admit for herself before anyone could do anything positive about it.

"If she says nothing's wrong, then nothing's wrong."

"You probably right." Reese agreed. She relaxed her tensed frame but held onto her worry.

"Did I already say how beautiful our daughter is?" Andre changed the tone of the conversation to pry the concerned look off of Reese's face before the wheels of her curiosity started to turn.

"She can't help it. She got her daddy's cute little nose and high cheekbones." Reese said admiring her daughter's features.

"Well, let's just hope she gets her mom's good, White-girl hair." Andre teased Reese about her mixed heritage; something he knew she couldn't stand. But the drowsy smile that briefly appeared on her daughter's face put her in too good a mood to be bothered by his comment.

"Yes, Lord!" Reese retaliated. "Cause if she gets your hair, you dealing with them naps!"

"Don't be hating!" Andre caressed his matted down, uneven afro. "You don't complain when you be running your fingers through all this."

"Aww, I'm sorry, Sweetie." Reese stroked Andre's hair and then caressed his cheek before leaning in to kiss his lips. Andre rested his head on her shoulder.

"Mama got two little babies." Reese said cradling her baby and her baby's daddy in her arms. But Andre interrupted the Kodak moment when he abruptly lifted from Reese's embrace.

"It's still one thing that's been bothering me about Adriana that I can't figure out."

His comment put Reese on alert as she pondered what would come out of his mouth next. She immediately thought he may have noticed something medically wrong with their child. She started examining the child herself trying to recall anything out of the ordinary she may not have overlooked.

"What's that, Baby?" She cringed to soften the blow of whatever he was about to say.

"Where the Hell you think she got them grey eyes from?"

Reese awoke to the sound of two Sports Center analysts discussing the details of some basketball player's arrest. Adriana was napping in her crib, and Andre was also sound asleep on the small visitor's couch that could only accommodate half of his long frame. One of his arms dangled off the side and almost touched the cold hospital floor, and both of his legs were cut off at the knee by the arm rest. His awkward position amused Reese and a laugh burst from her lips.

"What you laughing at?" Andre mumbled with his eyes still closed.

"How can you sleep like that?"

"I don't know 'cause my neck is killing me." Andre sat upright to relieve the ache building in the nape of his neck. He rubbed the spot with his hand to help ease the pain.

"Come here, Baby."

Andre walked over and sat on the edge of Reese's hospital bed. She massaged his neck and shoulders, but his grunts let her know his body needed more healing than her hands could give.

"Boo, you been here with me all day. Why don't you go home and get some rest?"

"What if you need something?"

"My mama can get it for me…" Reese looked around the room and realized her mother was not in it. "Where is she, anyway?"

"She said she needed to get to the liquor store before it closed."

"That figures. Guess we won't be hearing from her anytime soon." Reese knew her mother could not resist jumping at the first chance to have a cocktail and was probably at her apartment drunk and passed out on the couch.

"Yeah. She told me she would be back in the morning with breakfast. So, I think I should stay here to keep you company."

Andre had no interest in leaving the side of his fiancée and new baby no matter how tired or worn out he felt.

"If you wanna do something for me, you'll take your ass home and bring my bright-eyed, upbeat fiancé back here with you in the morning." Reese knew if Andre spent another night on that couch, he'd eventually fall into the grouchy attitude he got when he was sleep deprived; the attitude she could not stand and was not prepared to deal with two days out of labor.

Andre could tell that Reese was not going to back down. So he decided to make her happy and give in to her request.

"Okay, I'll go home." He turned around and gave Reese a goodbye hug and kiss. "But if you need anything, call me. I don't care what time it is. Alright?"

"Okay. You know I will. Now, get up outta here and let me bond with my baby." Reese playfully pushed him off of the bed and laughed.

"Yeah, yeah. You just don't forget who gave her to you, girl." Andre walked toward the door, and Reese was relieved when he closed it behind him. His words had reminded her that she really didn't know who had given her the child, and she didn't want him to notice the change in her mood that the worry had caused. He had already taken notice of the grey eyes that could have come from Terrance. And Reese hoped her partially true explanation about how grey eyes ran in her mother's side of the family would hold off his suspicions.

Reese's tortured thoughts were interrupted by the weak screech out of her baby's mouth. Her first thought was to call the nurse to tend to the crying infant, but her motherly instinct kicked in and she decided to step up and take care of it herself. She carefully cradled the infant close to her body and noticed that the child's wide-open wails calmed to a food-seeking suckle. She removed one side of her gown to breast feed, and, surprisingly, the child latched on without much difficulty. Tears formed in Reese's eyes. The realization that she could nurture and soothe her child with nothing more than her body was amazing. And the sight of her daughter's contentment in her arms was overwhelming.

Reese looked up to wipe the tears from her eyes and keep them from falling onto her daughter's face, and in her blurred vision stood a familiar shadow. She rubbed her eyes to see more clearly, and Terrance's grey gaze looked straight into them. He was holding an oversized teddy bear and a bushel of tulips.

"Terrance?" Reese clutched her daughter closer, trying to use the infant to cover her nakedness.

"What's up, Reese?" Terrance held his smiling gaze though he was overwhelmed by the sight of his former lover breast-feeding a baby.

"What you doing here?" Reese was struggling with the reality that he was actually standing in front of her.

"I came to see my little girl."

"How did you…?"

Reese's racing thoughts occupied her brain and kept her from being able to finish her sentence. His statement had confused her on so many levels. Not only did he know she was pregnant and that it was possibly his child, but he actually knew the baby's sex. Terrance took note of her weary expression and decided to ease her confusion. He sat the teddy bear and flowers down on the couch that was still warm from Andre's body heat before stating his case.

"After we broke up, I wanted to apologize for how it ended, but you wouldn't answer my calls...."

Reese had ignored his calls and texts after their breakup to focus her attention on her relationship with Andre. She knew having any contact with Terrance would only make her yearning for him grow stronger and build tension in her engagement.

"So I had my manager, Rick, find your mom's number, and she told me everything."

As Terrance continued to explain, it dawned on Reese that she should have confessed her pregnancy back in Dallas to avoid the awkward confrontation that was about to take place in Gulfport. She also cursed her mother's name for not telling her about his call. But on her second thought, she realized that her bitter mother had probably omitted the information to make her pay for her indiscretions.

"Don't be mad at your mom." Terrance seemed to read Reese's mind. "I told her not to tell you. I wanted this meeting to be a surprise...You surprised?"

Reese could feel the anger behind Terrance's happy façade, and butterflies built in her stomach.

"Look, Terrance, I'm sorry you had to find out like this...."

"When the fuck was you planning on telling me?" Terrance smile left the scene as his harsh scold interrupted the apology he did not want to hear. Reese was about to part her lips and try to explain, but Terrance continued to rant.

"Was you ever gonna tell me?"

"No, alright! I wasn't gonna tell you?" Reese blurted out her confession before he had a chance to interrupt her again. Her outburst caused Adriana to jump and wake up from her milk-induced coma. Reese removed her breast from the infant's mouth and hurried to cover her body from the heat of Terrance's searing eyes.

"Why not?" Terrance walked up to Reese and peeked at the wide-eyed child in her arms. His body tingled when he took in the smoky gaze and round face that was almost an exact replica of the infant in the baby pictures on his parents' mantle.

"Because she needs a father, not just a sperm donor, and I know Andre will be that for her."

"And you think I wouldn't?"

Her character assault stung Terrance's soul. He had been raised by a very-present father who had taught him the importance of being a real dad; a lesson he intended to live by with his own children.

"Well, I wasn't going to risk losing a sure thing with Andre to find out."

"So you was just gonna let some other nigga raise my child?"

"It's still a possibility that she ain't your child?

"Reese, look at her!" He growled. "You know that's my child."

"No, I don't." Reese was not willing to admit her own feelings that the child was most likely his.

"Well, we gonna find out 'cause I want a paternity test. And if it's my child, you're gonna leave that bum-ass nigga and move out to Dallas with me."

Reese did not appreciate his demanding attitude, even though she knew that was his personality. But just as she was about to put him in his place, she heard the door to the room creaking open.

"Hey, Boo, it's me. I got all the way home before I noticed I didn't have my wallet..."

Andre halted and his smile vanished when he was met with the vision of an unknown man standing too close for comfort to his fiancée and daughter. Upon closer examination, he realized the man before him was former USM football standout, Terrance Forrest. He immediately wondered why a pro football player was in Reese's room and looked to her for an explanation.

"Hey, Dre…This is Terrance." Reese stuttered.

"Yeah, I know who he is, but what the fuck he doing in here?"

Andre made his displeasure known with his tense stance and the slicing glare he used to dissect Terrance's face. His defensiveness amused Terrance, who countered his stare with an arrogant smile.

"He's my friend. He just came to see Adriana. Chill out."

Reese tried to calm Andre before he took his anger too far. She was slightly annoyed by his overreaction but knew he had far more reason than he knew to be upset.

"Yeah." Terrance chimed in. "I just came to congratulate my old buddy on her little bundle of joy. That's all."

He grabbed the teddy bear from the couch as evidence to the innocent intentions of his visit. Andre calmed down at the sight of the toy, realizing he was letting his jealousy get the best of him.

"My bad…." Andre started to apologize, but his apology was stopped cold when he took notice of the grey glimmer in Terrance's eyes. Suspicion of his worst fear built in his brain, but he pushed it to the back of his mind. He was not prepared to face what it implied.

"It's okay, Baby. Here's your wallet?"

Reese grabbed his wallet off the rolling dinner tray and waved it in his direction to distract his attention from Terrance's face. He looked at her with agonized eyes and nearly snatched the wallet out of her hand. He knew she was trying to rush him out of the awkward situation, but he was not about to leave her alone with the grey-eyed bandit.

"Hey, Man, it's getting late, and I know my girl is tired so I think it's time for you to go so she can get some rest."

"Alright then, Dawg." Terrance agreed, but his hard expression let Andre know he was not intimidated. He walked straight up to Andre and extended his hand.

"It was nice meeting you, Drew."

"It's Dre."

Andre reluctantly shook Terrance's hand, giving him the same scowl he wore when he first laid eyes on him.

"My fault…Dre." Terrance corrected himself while holding back the urge to snicker.

The way he was getting under Andre's skin still amused him, and his cocky smile returned before he released his firm grasp on his competitor's hand.

"Bye, Reese. Remember what I said." Terrance walked toward the door with Andre following close behind him.

"We'll talk later." Reese let Terrance know that his demands were still up for negotiation. She also knew the words would finally bring the nightmarish confrontation to an end.

"I'll look forward to it." Terrance pulled the door toward him but could not leave without landing one final blow to Andre's wounded ego.

"Bye Drew."

Chapter 11

Ryan walked through the doors of the Boiling Point and straight up to the booth where his accountant and business mentor, Frank Laneaux, was having a drink.

"It's a little early for liquor, ain't it?" Ryan smiled as he looked down at his watch that read 12:25 p.m.

"Boy, when you got a wife, three kids, and a girlfriend on the side, it ain't ever too early for bourbon." Frank flashed his pristine smile and raised his glass toward his client before taking another small sip. His thick Cajun accent lingered in the air like fog over the swamp waters near his childhood home in Lafayette, Louisiana.

"Let me get you something so you can join me in this drunk lunch." Frank started to raise his hand to get the waiter's attention.

"No, I'm cool. You said we needed to talk so let's talk." Ryan sat down across from Frank. His eyes were immediately drawn to the gleam of the diamond-studded cuff links on the sleeves of Frank's charcoal blazer. Frank saw that Ryan's attention was quickly retreating. But before he could open his mouth to bring his client back into the discussion, Ryan interrupted him.

"Damn, Frank, them diamonds blinding me. I must be paying you too much." Ryan laughed.

"Well, I don't know about all that, but you sure are putting too much into this here restaurant." Frank's eyes fell solemn as he shied away from Ryan's grin and ran his fingers through his short salt-and-pepper streaked curls.

"What you mean by that?" Ryan's grin was hampered by his accountant's revelation.

"I'm gonna give it to you straight, RT. The profits from this place are barely enough to cover its expenses, and if they keep falling like they been doing, the costs gonna start cutting into your club money."

"Well, what I need to do to fix it?" Ryan searched Frank's eyes for any glimmer of hope and braced himself when he found there was none.

"You need to cut your losses and shut this place down." Frank's blunt negativity threw Ryan, who was used to his accountant and business mentor only giving him positive feedback and advice.

"You don't have no other solution?" Frustration built inside of Ryan as he struggled to grasp the dark reality of the situation.

"Hey, I told you from the beginning not to open this place unless you were seriously committed."

"I am committed."

"How are you committed when you coming in here after 12 every day, nobody ever knows where you are when I call the office, and you let your damn chef open her own damn restaurant and steal all your clientele?"

The only part of Frank's scold that Ryan heard was about Saniyah abandoning ship and taking his customers. This sent his frustration into a quiet rage boiling underneath his skin. He knew he hadn't been the best manager, but there hadn't been any problems until Saniyah started doing her own thing. He thought.

"That bitch cost me my restaurant."

Ryan hid his anger from Frank and tried to focus his attention on saving his restaurant.

"What if we try to win the customers back?"

"How we gonna win them back when they came here for Saniyah's cooking in the first place?"

Ryan's refusal to give in was starting to irritate Frank. He pulled up his jacket sleeve to reveal how much wasted time had ticked off of his stainless-steel Cartier watch.

"Oh, what, you got somewhere else you need to be, Frank? It's funny how you got time to go spend my money on fancy watches and shit, but you ain't got time to help me keep my restaurant."

Ryan's audacious statement shocked Frank, but his shock was soon replaced with hurt that his long-time friend would make such harsh accusations against him.

"I didn't wanna go there with you, young blood, but since you took it to that level, I guess I'm gonna have to take you down a notch."

"Man, whatever."

Ryan folded his arms in defiance of his accountant's parental tone. He looked away from the piercing seriousness of Frank's 20-years-older eyes and sucked his teeth to show his displeasure with the direction of the conversation.

"Whatever all you want, but I cut my fee once I realized this place was tanking. I'm making enough with my other clients that I don't need your money. And since we were such good friends, I thought I'd help you out until your finances was stable. But I guess I was a fool to do that, huh?"

Frank's revelation wiped the disdain off of Ryan's face.

"Aww...Hey, man, I'm sorry. I didn't know..."

"Save your apologies for somebody that needs them." Frank cut Ryan's groveling short. "Now, what's this idea you got?"

"I was thinking we can do some kind of promotions campaign. You know, shoot a commercial or something like that." Ryan's eyes lit up as the possibilities filled his mind.

"No, no, no. That's just gonna add more expenses with no guarantee of any results. Besides, you don't have the high-caliber cooking anymore to hold onto the clients once you get them back."

"Well, what if I hire another hot chef?"

"Your budget ain't gonna stretch long enough for you to find somebody on Saniyah's level."

"How long do I have?"

"Look, Ryan, it's not gonna work so just shut the place down. If you close in the next two or three months and sell the building, you can come out of it with some extra cash and still have one profitable business going for you."

Frank's reasoning was starting to make sense to Ryan, especially since the idea bulb in his brain was starting to dim.

"Fine, Frank, you win. I'll sell." Ryan slumped over as a sign of surrender.

"Thank you." Frank exhaled a sigh of relief and relaxed the tense posture he had been holding since the conversation got heated.

"So, you think you can find me a buyer?"

"Do I look like a real estate agent to you, Boy? I'm already not getting paid for my services. Now, you want me to take on extra responsibilities."

"C'mon, Frank, help your boy out." Ryan's eyes begged his accountant for cooperation and support.

"Alright, I'll look through my contacts and see what I can do." Frank lifted up from the table, and Ryan followed suit.

"Thanks, Man." Ryan grabbed Frank's hand and pulled him in for a manly embrace.

"You know I got your back, young blood…But, look here, I gotta go take care of some business. I'll keep you posted if I come across a potential buyer."

Frank gave Ryan a pat on the back and a compassionate stare before releasing his grasp and starting for the door. Ryan watched his accountant make his way out of the building and did not move until he heard the revving engine of Frank's yellow Porsche.

Ryan walked to the bar and took a seat at the end. He raised a finger in the air to catch the bartender's attention.

"What can I get for you, Mr. Taylor?" The bartender's simple, customer service statement hit Ryan hard as he realized this man would soon be out of a job along with the other twenty-nine employees working in his dying establishment.

"Let me get bourbon on the rocks." Ryan knew the drink's slow burn was just the kind of sting he needed to forget the suffocating pain of failure and disappointment.

"What kind of bourbon would you like, Sir?" The smile on the bartender's face and his pleasant tone irritated Ryan. And he felt guilt swelling in his chest at the thought of what this man's face would look like when he announced the restaurant would be closing. The bartender was about to reiterate his question to break the awkward silence between himself and his boss, but Ryan choked back the emotion in his throat and gave an answer.

"The strongest you got, Man."

Chapter 12

Terrance pulled into the Gulf Villa apartment complex and parked his black and chrome Navigator in front of the complex playground. No children were in sight, but there were plenty of grown vagrants lounging on the recently-built recreational equipment. Terrance took in the scene with amazement that the grown men would deny children a place to play, all while providing them with a poor example of what to become. His first mind told him to make his feelings known, but his second mind reminded him that he was not in Dallas and that his .45 was locked in a box on his closet shelf.

Terrance started to turn off the ignition and exit his car, which was attracting more attention from the group of vagrants than he liked, but he realized that he did not know the building number he was seeking. His agent had provided the complex address and apartment number but had neglected to inform him of which of Gulf Villa's twenty buildings was the right one. Terrance reached for his phone and thumbed through his contacts to find his agent's number. He did not notice the old bum approaching his car on a pink Huffy mountain bike until the man was tapping on his driver side window.

"Hey, Boss man, you need a car wash? I'll do it for twenty bucks."

The bum's scratchy, slurred tone was muffled by the window. Terrance took his eyes off his phone and was amused by the sight of the six-foot, skin-and-bones, rag-clad stature of the man staring at him through bloodshot, half-opened eyes.

Terrance lowered the driver side window and his nostrils filled with the potent scent of Mad Dog 20/20. He winced and covered his nose with his hand to block the offensive smell.

"Do it look like this car need to be washed?" Terrance referenced the spotless, freshly-waxed vehicle.

"Well, just let me hold something then." The bum casually leaned his folded arms onto the window opening and revealed his near-toothless smile. Terrance pushed open the door to make the man back away from his vehicle. He exited the car and was met with the vision of the girl's bike and '70s-style vacuum cleaner, most likely boosted from their owners, that accompanied the intoxicated stranger. Terrance's silence and obvious intent to abandon the conversation, prompted the man to speak.

"C'mon, Boss man, help a brother out."

"Man, I ain't trying to support your habit."

The bum threw his head back in surprise at Terrance's assumption.

"Habit? I ain't got no habit. I just got outta rehab." He poked out his chest to show pride in the accomplishment.

"Well, it looks like you need to go back in, Player."

"Oh, you one of them stingy brothers, huh?"

The bum put his hands on his hips and berated Terrance with his glare. Terrance was about to walk away until he remembered he still didn't know where he was going.

"Look, Man, I'll give you the twenty if you can tell me where Reese Dixon lives."

"Reese Dixon?"

The bum scratched his grey chin whiskers in contemplation.

"Oh yeah, I know her. She stays right there." The bum pointed in the direction of Building 1 which was only a few feet away from Terrance's vehicle.

"You sure?" Terrance asked.

"Hell, yeah, I could never forget that face…or that *ass*!"

"Say what?"

Terrance balled up his fists and tensed his frame. The bum noticed his displeasure and raised his hands to cower away from Terrance's menacing posture.

"Oh, my bad, Boss man. You hitting that?"

"Mind your business." Terrance retrieved the money clip from his back pocket and pulled out a single twenty-dollar bill. He handed the currency to the bum, who immediately snatched it out of his hand.

"Whatever you say, Boss man."

The bum stuck the money into the front pocket barely hanging on to his tattered brown and black plaid button up. He mounted the pink bike and held up the peace sign before riding off in the opposite direction dragging the old vacuum behind him.

When the bum was a safe distance away, Terrance locked his car and activated the alarm. He walked up to Reese's apartment door and knocked. After a few moments, the door pulled open and Reese stood before him holding Adriana in her arms. Her eyes bucked when she looked up from her daughter's developing features and took in the full-grown frame she dreamed about every night.

"Terrance?"

"That's what they call me." Terrance smiled.

"What you doing here?" Reese found it hard to hold on to her astonishment and fight off the desire to react to his smile with one of her own.

"I came to see my little girl." Terrance looked down at the wide-eyed fussy infant squirming in her mother's arms. Reese retrieved the pacifier that was clipped to Adriana's Onesie and put it into her daughter's mouth. She rocked the infant to settle her down. The child's cries fell silent and her face relaxed.

"Terrance, you know I'm with Andre. You can't just be showing up here all unannounced."

Reese's scold brought Terrance's attention back to her. Despite the caution in her words, Terrance stepped forward. His approach forced

Reese to step back into the house, allowing him to enter.

"That nigga here or something?" Terrance surveyed the apartment as far as his eyes could see.

"No, but if he was…"

"But he ain't so hush up and let me hold my daughter." Terrance interrupted Reese's frame of mind, and she handed her child over to him without thought. Terrance walked over and sat down on the sofa cradling the baby like priceless merchandise. Reese put her freed up hands on her hips and sucked her teeth.

"You need to stop that."

"Stop what?"

Terrance kept his googly eyes on Adriana. He blew air kisses and made silly faces at the infant, who looked straight into his face with bright-eyed curiosity.

"You don't know if she's yours or not."

"Reese, stop lying to yourself, Baby. The girl looks just like me." Terrance's eyes still did not move away from Adriana's face.

"So what? Looks can be deceiving." That time, Terrance looked up and stared straight into Reese's eyes.

"Yeah, well, them test results won't be."

"I'm not doing no DNA test." Reese folded her arms and turned away from Terrance's stare. He stood up and walked toward her, carefully juggling Adriana.

"Why the hell not?"

"'Cause I don't wanna hurt Andre." Reese's mention of the name made Terrance cringe.

"Again with this Andre nigga."

Reese noticed her daughter's head drooping in Terrance's arms. Her eyes were locked tight and her mouth was suckling an imaginary nipple, as the real pacifier dangled from her body. Reese took her daughter from Terrance and started walking toward her room. Terrance followed close behind her.

Reese put Adriana in her crib as soon as she got into the room, and the child fell straight to sleep with the pacifier returned to her mouth. Terrance stopped at the door and leaned against the frame with his arms folded watching Reese care for the child. Reese looked at the pissed off expression on his face and knew her comment had sparked the jealousy in him.

"Look, Terrance, you gonna have to accept the fact that Andre is my fiancé, and we're getting married. He's gonna be Adriana's daddy, and that's just how it's gonna be."

"Not if me and my lawyer have anything to do with it." Terrance's matter-of-fact tone and the audacity of his comment shocked Reese.

"You and your lawyer can kiss my ass." Reese's tone was sharp, and her posture was even stronger. She waved her finger in the air and rolled her neck and eyes before returning her hands to her hips. Her hood stance amused Terrance, and a smile stretched across his face from ear to ear as he thought of a response.

"Bend over, and I will." His devilish grin was contagious. Reese could not fight the urge to smile, but she managed to hold it to a smirk.

"I'm not joking, Terrance."

Reese turned away from him and leaned against the rail of Adriana's crib. She looked down at the sleeping infant trying to remove the smile from her face and the romantic thoughts brewing in her mind. Terrance walked up behind her and put his arms around her waist.

"I know, Boo. I'm just trying to lighten the mood. You getting all hostile on me."

"'Cause I'm serious...And don't think you gonna snuggle all up on me and get me to bend to your will either." Reese's words were contradicted by her actions.

Terrance's embrace was too warm and too familiar for her to resist. She allowed her body to melt into his as if the drama between them had never happened.

"Well, what if I do this?" Terrance slid his hand underneath Reese's short pink and white-striped Polo dress. He put his hand between her body and the small fabric of her thong and massaged between her legs. Reese closed her eyes and an unexpected moan burst from her lips. She leaned over Adriana's crib in pure ecstasy.

Terrance continued his handiwork and leaned down

over her to kiss her neck. Reese's eyes slowly

opened and returned her to reality. She took in the

sight of her daughter's innocence below and felt

embarrassed. She stood straight up and pushed

Terrance's hand off of her. She turned to face him

and pushed him back to create space between them.

"Why you pushing me away?"

"'Cause I don't belong to you."

Reese's gaze was stern. Seeing her child

had reminded her of the decision she made while

Adriana was still in her belly to stand by Andre.

Terrance grabbed Reese's hand, noticing her ring

finger finally held a small gold band and inferior

quality diamond.

"That nigga might have your hand, but I'm

gonna always have your heart." Terrance leaned

into Reese's ear and whispered, "And you know I got them panties on lock."

"Damn!" Reese thought.

Terrance's sultry baritone and the memory of his recent touch had her womanhood throbbing. She felt like her body heat was rising with every glance into Terrance's enticing grey gaze. She unfastened all the buttons on her dress and pulled the fabric back and forth to create a faint breeze of air over her body.

"What's wrong, Boo?" Terrance smiled. Reese's disposition let him know he was getting to her.

"I want you so bad I can taste you." Reese grabbed Terrance's T-shirt with both hands and pulled him into a long-anticipated lip lock. Terrance pulled his face away from Reese's kiss and grasped her head with both hands.

"What you doing?" Reese asked.

"You know I been dying to see what else that mouth can do."

Terrance rubbed his thumb gently over her soft, full lips. Reese took his hand and pulled him toward the bed. She pushed him down onto the mattress and bent over to give him a single kiss on the forehead before getting down on her knees.

Reese unzipped his jeans and pulled his erection out of the slit in his boxers. She massaged it with her hands a few times before giving it the Popsicle treatment. Terrance's leg jerked. He knew Reese was experienced, but he was not expecting such a talented performance. Once the tension of shock subsided, his body relaxed into the pleasure he was feeling. He fell back onto the mattress and put his hands behind his head, admiring the up and down movement of Reese's hair. But it wasn't long before he felt left out of the action. He sat back up and grasped the back of Reese's head. He gripped her short curls and used his clutch to guide her movement. His head fell back and his eyes closed.

When he looked up again, Andre was standing in the doorway with fire in his eyes. Terrance smiled at his hated rival with the same cocky grin he gave on their first meeting. He let Reese continue, not alerting her to Andre's presence.

"Reese, what the fuck?" Andre barked as he yanked Reese from the floor by her arm.

"Andre?... I'm sorry..." Reese's eyes bucked out of her head as she realized she was caught.

"*Sorry?*" Andre tightened his grip on Reese's arm and looked at her with bouncing, rage-filled eyes. Reese winced in the pain of Andre's clutches.

"You need to take your hands off my girl, Home boy."

Terrance stood up from the bed without pulling up his pants. Andre turned his rage in Terrance's direction. He released Reese's arm and used that same hand to punch Terrance in the jaw. The blow knocked Terrance off his balance, and he fell down onto the mattress. Andre jumped on top of him, and the two commenced to tussle and struggle to gain supremacy over the other.

"Andre, stop!" Reese screamed and pulled Andre's shoulder in an attempt to stop the fight. Andre looked back at her and pushed her away. When he turned back to face his opponent, the space between his eyes met Terrance's fist. Andre's unconscious body slumped down to the floor. Reese hovered over him and cradled his head in her arms. Terrance lifted from the bed and pulled up his pants. He looked from Reese's teary gaze to her fiancé's limp frame, rubbing his jaw to ease the ache from Andre's blow.

"When you ready to take the test, let me know." Terrance walked out the bedroom and exited the apartment. To avoid anymore drama, Reese waited until she heard her front door slam before she tried to revive Andre. She repeatedly slapped Andre's face until he was conscious.

"You alright?" The worry was written across Reese's face.

"Get the fuck off me, Trick." Andre pulled away from Reese's embrace and lifted to his feet. He looked down at her wide, glossy eyes in pure disgust before starting for the bedroom door. But before he was out of the room, he stopped mid-stride and turned back to face Reese.

"Just let me know one thing before I go."

"What?" Reese's voice cracked.

"Is Adriana mine?"

Reese could not bear to utter the 'I don't know' that would break his heart so she left his question unanswered. Her silence was enough to wound his soul, and tears welled up in his eyes. The rest of his face held on to the disgust he aimed at Reese as hard as the punch he had just taken.

"I'm out." He barked. "And I won't be back."

Chapter 13

July

A month after the altercation between Andre and Terrance, Reese sat with an envelope in her lap. She examined its smooth, white exterior with her hands reluctant to open it. She sucked in a soothing breath to calm her nerves before wedging her index finger between the envelope and its opening flap. She pulled the paper out, pulled apart its folds and read the truth she could no longer deny: Terrance was Adriana's father.

Reese's eyes misted over as she released the letter from her grasp. It slid out of her lap and fluttered down to the floor. Her face fell into her hands, and the emotion overflowed into her palms.

She felt the cold metal of her engagement ring pressing into her forehead. She took her hands down to examine the broken symbol of her fidelity to Andre. She twisted it off of her finger and sat it on the end table next to her. She no longer felt worthy enough to wear it.

Guilt along with the anxiety of the difficult call she had to make tightened in her throat. But she knew whether she made the call sooner or later, the outcome would be the same. So she took another soothing breath before pressing the send button on her cell phone. It rang twice and went straight to voicemail. So she waited for the beep to leave her message.

"Hey, um, Andre, I got the test results, and…" Reese burst into tears and took the phone away to regain her composure. Her voice was still shaky when she resumed her message. "She's not yours…So I know I probably won't hear from you in a while, but whenever you're ready to discuss this, give me a call. I am so sorry, Dre. And I, uh, want you to know that I still love you. And as crazy as this probably sounds, I never meant for any of this to happen. I hope to talk to you soon. Bye."

Reese hung up the phone and returned her soaking face to her palms. She cried for what seemed like an eternity until her daughter's hunger-driven screams disrupted her tortured tears. She retrieved Adriana from her crib and returned to her spot on the couch.

As she was preparing to breastfeed the frantic infant, she heard a knock on the front door. To Adriana's dismay, Reese redressed and went to answer it. The denied infant continued her screams until her mother silenced them with the pacifier. Reese opened the door and was met with Andre's stone cold face. He looked away from her weary, apologetic pout and the crying infant in her arms. His chest caved in with emotion, but he hid his pain with a cold, uncaring tone.

"I got your message, and I just came to get my ring back. I'll get my other stuff later."

"Alright." Reese retrieved the ring from the end table without another word. Andre was calm, and she wanted to keep him that way as long as possible. He took the ring from her outstretched hand and turned to walk back to his car. Reese was not expecting him to leave so abruptly and knew she would have to make the first move.

"Andre, don't you think we need to talk?"

Andre stopped and turned to face her. He stretched his hands out and his cold face turned sour.

"What the fuck you wanna talk about, Reese? Huh? You wanna talk about why you had some other nigga's dick in your mouth, or you wanna talk about how that nigga is the father of the baby you tried to fool *me* into believing was mine?"

His tone was so harsh and so unfamiliar to Reese that it made tears well in her eyes. She clutched her daughter close as if trying to protect her from Andre's hurtful scold.

"Andre, please!" Reese's voice was laced with pain.

"Please what? Please forgive you for ruining my life?" Andre's yell caught the attention of the playground vagrants and anyone else in range of the heated conversation. All eyes, including Andre's, were on Reese, awaiting her response.

"I'm sorry." Reese looked down to the cement walk way in shame.

"No you ain't. You probably happy that nigga's the father. Now your little gold-digging ass can have whatever you want. Congratulations!"

"It's not like that." Even after all she had put him through Reese was hurt that Andre thought so low of her character.

"Oh, it's not?" Andre gave her a knowing glare.

"No. It was never about money." Reese knew her words were only half true, but thought it best to be dishonest under the circumstances.

"Then what was it about? He bigger than me?" Andre tugged on the belt buckle holding up his sagging jeans. Small chuckles floated in the audience that both failed to notice gathering behind them.

"No…. Damn it, Andre. I don't love you."

Reese did not mean to be so harsh in her words and her tone, but the shock on Andre's face let her know she could not take it back.

"I mean, I thought that I could force myself to love you more than a friend, but I couldn't."

"So instead of telling me that from the jump and avoiding all this, you decide to string me along and deceive me? Look at all the damage you done!"

"I know. If I could, I would take it all back, but all I can do is apologize." Reese's face begged for forgiveness.

"Well, apology not accepted." Andre illustrated his biting rejection by turning to walk away.

"Andre, wait." Reese's painful plea irritated his ears, but Andre stopped and turned around.

"What?"

"I know you hate me, and rightfully so, but don't take it out on Adriana." Reese lifted the resting infant into his view. "I know how much you care for her, and I still want you to be a part of her life."

"But she ain't mine remember? Let that other nigga raise her." Andre turned his vision away from the beautiful little girl he could no longer call his own. He fought back the urge to cry out, realizing she was still the love of his life.

"I'm not asking you to raise her. I just know you love her, and I want you to keep on loving her." Reese's voice reminded Andre of the pain she had caused, and the compassion he was feeling for Adriana quickly morphed into the anger he felt toward her mother.

"I guess you should've thought about that before you laid down with another man."

The vision of Reese going down on Terrance entered Andre's head and made him wince to hold back his desire to strike her.

"Damn it, Reese, I lost my fiancée and my daughter all at once. Do you know how much that shit hurts? Huh? Do you?"

The boom of his voice and the crazed look in his eyes paralyzed Reese into a cowering statue.

"And now you want me to still come around like everything is okay. What kind of fool you take me for?"

"I know you're hurting, Andre. And I'm not asking you to decide right now. But if you do choose to stay in her life, I want you to be her Godfather."

Andre could not believe what he was hearing. A few weeks ago, he was the father. Now he was being downgraded to the almost meaningless role of Godfather. He still wanted to be in Adriana's life, but it was too soon for him to even think about being around Reese any longer than necessary.

"Godfather, huh? Well, I'll have to think on that one. 'Cause right now I got things to do like trying to get my money back for this stupid ring and canceling all these fucking wedding arrangements we made. But once I'm done with all that, I'll let you know."

Andre's sarcasm rolled off of Reese's back. She expected his participation in her daughter's life would not come without some hostility and was prepared for insults.

"Okay. I'll be waiting."

Reese's agreeable tone let Andre know his comment had failed to sting the way he intended. He could also see in her eyes that she was serious so he planned to give her request some thought. But he was not about to make her aware that she had gained any ground. He maintained his cold face and defiant posture.

"You do that. Later."

Reese sat in the gazebo outside of the Oasis Hotel and stared down at the half-eaten turkey sub she got from the break room vending machine. Her hour-long lunch break was nearing the mid-way point so she gave up on the soggy sandwich and balled it up inside a paper towel before tossing it into a nearby trashcan. She was not about to let the sad excuse for a meal be the highlight of her lunch. There was a greater mission to be achieved.

She had decided to wait a day before telling Terrance about the DNA results so that the sting of her confrontation with Andre would have time to wear off. She figured her conversation with Terrance would be a lot more joyful, and she wanted to be able to experience some satisfaction with the closure of her baby-father mystery.

Reese pulled her cell phone out of her purse and dialed Terrance's number. His phone rang twice before he picked up.

"What up, Girl?" Terrance's baritone played over the receiver and made Reese's knees buckle. She squatted down to take a seat on the edge of the sidewalk.

"I got good news." Reese smiled and butterflies formed in her stomach as she paused for a few seconds to build up his anticipation.

"Well, stop stalling and give it to me." Terrance blurted.

"The results came back. You're Adriana's dad."

Terrance sat back in his computer chair and stared in awe at the glow of the laptop screen on his desk.

"I knew it."

Terrance disguised his astonishment with confidence. He had the feeling Adriana was his from the moment Reese's mother told him about the pregnancy, but the verification of his hunch was still mind-blowing.

"Well, now I know it, too."

"So how old boy take the news?"

"We broke up." The smile Reese had been wearing through their entire conversation quickly fell into a solemn pout as she was reminded of the devastated state of her relationship with Andre. Terrance noticed the displeasure in her tone, but news of the break up was music to his ears.

"Good…I mean…I'm sorry to hear that, Boo." Terrance sympathetic tone was shrouded in insincerity. But his weak attempt to mask it amused Reese and the smile returned to her face.

"Yeah right. You ain't sorry."

"I know." Terrance's comedic compassion mellowed into genuine care. "But for real, are you okay?"

"Yeah. I feel bad about how everything went down, but I can't take it back. So I'm just gonna have to deal with the consequences of my actions and move on."

The words were therapeutic to Reese's soul as they left her lips. And the relief of letting her feelings out to a somewhat neutral party eased the guilt weighing on her mind.

"Aww. You want Daddy to come down there and make you feel better?" Terrance smiled and swiveled around in his computer chair. Reese could feel Terrance's sly smirk coming through the phone and sucked her teeth to hide her arousal.

"I want *Daddy* to come down here and help take care of his daughter."

"Now you know I'll be out there every chance I get until I'm able to get ya'll out here with me."

"Boy, please. I know your woman ain't about to have that."

"My woman? What woman?" Terrance sat straight up in his chair as confusion crept across his face.

"Don't play, Terrance. The little skeezer had you putting me up in a hotel."

"You talking about, Denise?"

"Yeah, that's her. What she gonna think about you shacking up with your baby's momma?"

Reese folded her arms and poked her lips in an

accusing pout as if Terrance were standing right in

front of her.

"Girl, I made all that up to make you mad.

She doesn't even exist." Terrance laughed and

relaxed his body back into the comforts of the

reclining chair.

"Seriously?" Reese was not sure whether to

believe him or not. Her adulterous past had inspired

her own slight distrust in the fidelity of others.

"Yeah. I was pissed off when I realized you

was choosing old dude over me so I came up with

something to try to hurt you as much as I was

hurting. I know it was childish, but that's all I

could come up with at the time."

Terrance's confession was doused in the

pain he felt when he and Reese called it quits. The

anger and anguish in his tone let her know his claim

was sincere and that his love for her was far deeper than she thought. An unintended smile stretched across her face, and an inappropriate giggle snuck out of her mouth.

"What's so funny?"

"In some twisted way, it's actually kind of sweet that your feelings for me made you go to such lengths to make me jealous."

The two shared a laugh, but their laughter soon lowered into an unusual, awkward silence. Both wanted to hear those three little words from the other and confess their own devotion. But both were too afraid of the rejection they would face if the person on the other end of the line no longer held the same feelings.

Reese had already burned Terrance once, and he was determined to tame his impulsive emotions and take the second approach slowly to make things work with his daughter's mother. And Reese was still reeling from the blows of her own infidelity because of her willingness to ignore her better judgment and jump the love gun with Andre. His love had driven her into the arms of another man, and she did not want that to happen with Terrance.

The silence was making Terrance anxious, and he knew Reese was probably just as uncomfortable. So he redirected the situation back to their earlier conversation.

"So how soon can you be in Dallas?" Terrance knew with Reese around him 24-7 it would be hard to maintain a causal relationship, but he felt his willpower and the life he wanted for his daughter were motivation enough to keep him on the slow, steady track.

"You really want me to come live with you?"

"Why wouldn't I?"

"I haven't exactly been the best candidate to have a relationship with lately."

Reese thought about the lies and heart break she had put both Andre and Terrance through and felt unworthy of the affection of either man.

"Look. I ain't like that sensitive ass nigga, Andre." Just as those words left Terrance's mouth, Andre beeped in on Reese's second line, but she ignored his call to focus on Terrance.

"He was too weak to tame you. But I know what you need to be satisfied."

"And what's that?"

"Hard dick and long money."

The bold statement left Reese absolutely speechless. Her knees buckled once again, and her thighs yearned for his separation. Those few words proved this man knew her body and her mind, and the crucifix he sometimes wore around his neck meant he must have shared her spirit, too. She thought, "*What else do I need to prove to myself that I love this man?*"

"I got you shook over there, huh?" Terrance boasted.

But Reese was wrapped up so tight within her own thoughts and emotions that the only response she could give was a lackluster chuckle. Terrance was about to probe for the reason behind her cold response, but he was interrupted by the buzz of his security system alerting him to a visitor's presence. He looked to the camera and saw the harsh scowl of his personal trainer piercing straight into his soul. He looked down at the time on his laptop and realized he was late for his fitness session. He commenced to bombard Reese with his closing arguments, leaving no room between sentences for her input.

"Damn, Boo, I'm late for my training session. But, look, you don't gotta make up your mind about Dallas right now. We can talk about it next time I come to visit. But in the meantime, be on the lookout for a call from my manager, Rick. I'm gonna have him set up an account for you and Adriana. Thanks for calling to tell me the good news. Kiss Adriana for me. Gotta go. Bye."

Before Reese had a chance to respond, Terrance was gone off of the line. His absence gave her instant courage to say what she could not manage before, praying some way he would still hear her declaration.

"I love you, too."

Reese smiled and looked down at the pink leather watch on her wrist. The timepiece read 1:25 p.m., five minutes before her lunch break would come to an end. She started to walk toward the break room to clock in and heard the voicemail alert go off on the phone. So she hit the send button to dial her mail box and waited patiently for the operator to replay the messages as she made her way inside the hotel.

"Hey, Reese, this is Dre. I was just calling to let you know that I thought about what you said, and I realized that I do still want to be in Adriana's life. I would love to be her Godfather if the offer still stands. It's probably gonna take a while before me and you can be cool like we were, but I'm willing to work on it for Adriana. I still love both of you and can't see my life without either one of you in it. So whenever you get this message, just give me a call so we can talk."

Chapter 14

August

Saniyah walked into Ryan's condo and was met with the same greeting she had come home to every night for weeks. Ryan sat slumped on the couch aiming the remote at the television, which he constantly flipped from one sports channel to the next. His expression was a nonchalant droop credited to the two empty beer bottles and watered down, half-empty cocktail glass on the coffee table beside his propped up feet.

The only new addition to the scene was his choice of clothing. The royal blue-striped button up, crease-pressed navy slacks, and black Cole Haan Venetian slip-ons were a far cry from the worn out boxers and stretched wife beaters he was usually wearing when Saniyah got home.

Ryan paid Saniyah's entrance no mind. He continued to stare blankly at the television screen and only tore his eyes from its glow to focus on taking another sip of his cognac. His disinterest in her presence and newfound lack of motivation annoyed Saniyah, but she usually ignored his apathy to avoid confrontation.

That night she had had enough. Instead of going straight to bed, Saniyah walked from the door to stand beside Ryan, who continued to ignore her. She stared down at him as if trying to burn a whole through his forehead with her eyes. She was tired of allowing their relationship to crumble and was determined to break Ryan out of the negative walls he was building between them.

"What?"

The word burst from Ryan's lips suddenly as he jumped out of his sedentary slump and pierced her stare with aggravated eyes. Saniyah's heart jumped in fear, but her body held firm.

"Hey to you, too."

She put her hands on her hips and sucked her teeth to cover her discomfort in a veil of confidence. Ryan's body relaxed back into its slothful position, and his eyes darted back to the final seconds of the Cavaliers-Celtics game.

"What up?"

Ryan's focus remained straight ahead. He had no intention of listening to whatever conversation followed. But he knew his show of interest would keep Saniyah's nagging at bay.

Saniyah calmed her firm stance and reached into the large zebra-print handbag clutching her shoulder. She pulled out a small Styrofoam container wrapped in a plastic bag and sat her purse on the couch beside Ryan.

"I brought you some gumbo. You want me to warm it up for you?" Saniyah's offer had more to do with love than hunger. Her food always seemed to bring them together, and gumbo was Ryan's favorite meal.

"No. I already ate."

Ryan's lie was in rebellion to Saniyah's success. His stomach yearned for the seafood-filled aroma resonating from the container, but he refused to eat anything that came from her restaurant.

"You sure?" Saniyah's face twisted with shock.

"Yeah, I'm sure!"

Aggravation re-illustrated Ryan's expression, and his tone followed suit. That time, Saniyah could not conceal her fear. She jumped away from his bark and swiftly made her way into the kitchen to be a safe distance from his wrath.

"When you gonna stop with the attitude?" Saniyah found courage in the space between them.

"What attitude?"

Ryan held his aggravated tone but kept most of his attention out of the conversation. He was in no mood to argue and wished they could return to the silence that had been between them for the past few weeks.

"The attitude you been giving me ever since you found out you had to close the Boiling Point."

Although Ryan had never mentioned it, Saniyah knew that it was the reason for his disgruntled disposition and his animosity toward her.

"Well, maybe I'm giving you attitude 'cause you the reason why."

Ryan sat straight up on the couch and gave full, snake-eyed attention to Saniyah. His accusation was bitter. He had held it in so long that it had started to fester in his spirit. The release was relieving, but the venom with which it came was harsh.

"You need to stop blaming me and take responsibility for your own failure."

Saniyah immediately went on the defensive and spit venom of her own. Her stare was firm and just as potent as her romantic rival.

"Say what?"

The aggravation in Ryan's tone was replaced with rage. He lifted from the couch and slowly stalked toward Saniyah with both hands on his hips and his head cocked to the left with confusion.

"Look at you…at home pouting when you need to be at the club making sure *its* doors stay open."

Saniyah's words were strong, but her body tensed with every step Ryan took toward her. Still she was determined to stand her ground and express her feelings so she continued her rant.

"Maybe if you put half the time you spend chasing hoes into handling your business, your restaurant would still be a success without me."

Saniyah's insult cut Ryan deep. He ignored all truth in the hate-filled statement and was consumed with the need for revenge. He walked toward Saniyah until they were standing face to face, and his expression twisted into a scowl fit for his worst enemy.

"Well, maybe if you weren't such a poor excuse for a girlfriend, I wouldn't need to chase other women."

The ease with which the words rolled off his tongue shocked Saniyah and anger filled her veins. Without any thought, she cocked her right hand back and slammed her palm into Ryan's cheek. His face jerked to the other side and the point of impact reddened in his manila skin.

Fear spread across Saniyah's face as she realized what she had done. She started to back away, but her retreat was halted by Ryan's sudden grasp around her neck. He pushed her body into the kitchen wall and squeezed her throat tighter once she was stationary.

"Bitch, are you crazy? What I tell you about putting your fucking hands on me?"

Saniyah's eyes pleaded for release as she gasped for air, but her pleas went unanswered. Ryan balled his empty hand into a fist and pounded it into Saniyah's right side. Tears slid down her checks and rolled onto the hand holding her captive. She tried unsuccessfully to maneuver her body out of the path of his blows, but her strength weakened with every second of air she lost and every hit she took. She felt her consciousness slipping away. The face of her attacker went in and out of focus. She thought.

"He's going to kill me!"

Abruptly, the blaring sound of Ryan's ringtone, Rick Ross' "Hustlin," ended the assault. Ryan released Saniyah as if the fight had never happened and walked away. Saniyah slumped down to the floor and rested her head on top of her knees. She struggled to catch her breath through her cries inspired by the throbbing pain aching its way up the side of her body.

Ryan stood with his back facing Saniyah. He pulled his cell phone from his pants pocket and smiled as he read the name, "Nessa," on the screen. He took in a few deep breaths to calm down from the adrenaline rush of the altercation before answering the call.

"What up, Girl?"

"Hey, Baby. You on your way yet?"

"I was just getting ready to walk out the door."

"Don't keep me waiting too long, Mr. Taylor."

"I won't. I'll be there in a minute."

Ryan hung up the phone and put it back into his pants pocket. He walked straight to the door, grabbing his keys from the coffee table as he passed it. Before exiting, he stopped and slightly turned his face so that he could see Saniyah's broken body in the corner of his eye.

"You lucky I got somewhere more important to be, Girl. I got a date with a *real* woman...so don't wait up."

Reese stood over Adriana's crib, watching the infant settle into sleep. She patiently waited for her daughter's tensed arms to relax and fall to her sides. Then she climbed into her own bed. She made the Sign of the Cross and said an Our Father before snuggling under her comforter. Soon her own arms were dangling lifelessly from the side of her bed as she drifted into sleep.

But Reese's peaceful slumber was short-lived. As soon as her mind started forming the beginning images of a dream, the cell phone on her night stand started to ring. Her eyes burst open and were immediately drawn to the bars of Adriana's crib. But the ring had not disturbed the infant, who was still sleeping soundly. So Reese cleared her throat and answered the call.

"Hello."

"Hey, Reese. It's Saniyah."

Saniyah was calling from the emergency waiting room of Memorial Hospital. Her voice sounded weak and sorrowful and scared Reese out of her relaxed position. She sat up in the bed as concern wrinkled in her brow.

"Hey, Girl. What's up?"

"I'm sorry to bother you this late, but…"

Saniyah suddenly cried out. The eyes of the elderly couple cuddling nearby were immediately drawn in her direction. She cowered away from their stares and carefully maneuvered her pain-ravaged body to face the opposite direction. Her next words were barely audible over her whimpers.

"I need you."

"Niyah, what's wrong?"

"I'm at the hospital."

The words sent shivers through Reese's body and caused a panic in her thought process. Every negative scenario played in her mind.

"Hospital? What happened?"

"Me and Ryan had a fight, and he…"

Saniyah's voice returned to the painful howl. She waited for the rush of emotion to subside before continuing her explanation.

"He cracked my ribs."

"He did what? Are you okay?"

"Yeah. I'm in a lot of pain, but the doctor told me I'll be fine in a few weeks."

Reese breathed a sigh of relief, and her demeanor quickly traveled from concern to vengeance.

"Where's Ryan? Is he there with you?"

"No. I don't know where he is. He left after the fight."

"He left you?"

"Yeah."

"You wait 'til I find his ass." Reese's fists tightened and her eyes squinted with rage.

"No, Reese. I don't want any more drama with him. I just want it to be over. Can you come and get me? I'm at Memorial."

Saniyah leaned over the rail of her chair to redistribute the pressure building under her bruises to the unharmed side of her body.

"Of course I'll come get you, Girl. But what you mean by anymore drama? Has he done this before?"

"Yeah." Saniyah's response was reluctant. She did not intend to tell Reese about the previous altercations.

"Oh my God! Niyah, why didn't you tell me?"

Reese's voice roared through the receiver and pierced Saniyah's ears. She pulled the phone away and closed her eyes in shame. Tears slid out of her clamped eyelids as she searched the darkness for an appropriate response.

"I was embarrassed."

Her throat ached as the painful words struggled to free themselves from her lips. She braced herself for judgment.

"Embarrassed?"

"You're always so strong and assertive with men. I figured you would think I was a punk for letting all this go on."

"Girl, please. You think a nigga ain't never tried to put his hands on me."

The nonchalant tone with which Reese spoke shocked Saniyah even more than the revelation. She searched her mind for any recollection of her cousin ever mentioning an abusive boyfriend and quickly realized she had none.

"Really? Who?"

"It ain't important. Just some nigga thought he was gonna solve my commitment issues with his fists."

Reese's face twisted in disgust as her mind filled with the memory of her former abuser's evil smirk.

"How did you handle it?"

Saniyah listened with open ears and wide-eyed curiosity, hoping her cousin's experience would help her deal with her own.

"I had my other man beat his ass."

The two cousins shared a laugh before the solemnity of the situation returned their conversation to uncomfortable silence. Both contemplated their victimization in the quiet; Reese amused by the irony of her solution and Saniyah saddened by her failure to be as savvy.

"You always got an answer for everything." Saniyah's somber tone narrated her broken spirit.

"That's why you should've told me sooner. I could've had Ryan's ass taken care of before it even got to this point."

Reese's words made Saniyah realize her cousin's stint with abuse had filled her with animosity toward all abusive men. Saniyah did not want to share these same feelings and was determined to handle her own situation without violence.

"But I don't want to hurt him."

"Why not? He hurt you."

"I know, but..."

Reese interrupted Saniyah's spineless reasoning. She was determined to make Ryan feel the pain he had caused her cousin.

"But what?" Reese paused as it became clear why Saniyah did not want to hurt her attacker. "I know you not seriously still feeling this dude."

"I don't know."

Saniyah gave a half-hearted response, realizing her cousin had read the truth behind her hesitance. Part of her still desired to be with Ryan. She knew underneath all of his viciousness that he still cared about her and was optimistic that they could be happy together if he got help for his anger problems.

"Niyah, you in an emergency room now because of him. This time it was just cracked ribs...but next time, he might crack your skull. You willing to risk your life to be with him?"

Reese brought up the mortality of the situation. With her cousin's fragile state, she did not want to be so harsh, but Saniyah's obvious intent to ignore the worst-case scenario inspired the fiery reprimand.

The words hit home with Saniyah. Her mind flashed back to the terrifying altercation. She remembered the hatred in Ryan's eyes, in his voice, and in his force. Her eyes misted over, and she rubbed the bruises on her neck that outlined the imprint of his choking grip. Not only had this man tried to beat life out of her, but he had also tried to deny her the ability to take life in. She realized, whether Ryan meant it or not, every move he made against her was designed to kill. And there was no love in murder.

"You know, I really felt like he was going to kill me this time. If he hadn't left to be with his other woman, he probably would have."

"Other woman? This fool hitting you and cheating on you, too?"

Reese practically jumped out of her skin as she leaped from her bed. She illustrated her outrage with a waving finger and rolling neck.

"Oh no. This stops now. You moving back in with me for good this time, and I'm not taking no for an answer."

Saniyah was all for Reese's declaration. The flash back had given her an epiphany. Ryan did not and would not ever love her the way she wanted or deserved. So the only solution was exodus.

"You right. It's time for me to end this." The newfound boldness in Saniyah's voice excited Reese and a smile relaxed the anger her face had been holding for the entire conversation. She could sense that her words had achieved their intended purpose and was pleased with the determination in her cousin's tone.

"That's what I'm talking about, Girl. And don't you ever keep something like this from me again."

"I won't..."

Saniyah paused. Her confident air wavered as her thoughts drifted from overcoming her current oppressor to having her former dictator find out about her captivity.

"While we on the topic of keeping secrets, can you not mention this to your mother. I don't want my mom knowing anything about this."

"My lips are sealed." Reese's clichéd promise was not convincing.

"I'm for real, Reese." Saniyah spoke with assertive passion.

Reese had no intention to go against her word, but she understood her cousin's concern since her reputation for secrecy was nonexistent. Still she had her own reasons to keep the situation under wraps.

"I don't want your mama knowing I let her little girl come over here and get all banged up. She already doesn't like me."

Reese cringed at the thought of the disapproving nose her aunt turned up every time she saw her and shuddered to think what this look would become if she found out about the abuse.

"What you talking about? My mom loves you." Saniyah lied.

Even though she knew Reese had some idea of the truth, her mother's distaste for her cousin had never left the intimacy of immediate family conversation.

"Well, I'm sure she'll hate me if she finds out the man I introduced you to been beating your ass on the regular..."

Reese choked on her words. Her face flushed with emotion and tears formed in her eyes.

"Saniyah, I am so sorry for hooking you up with that bastard."

"It's not your fault. You didn't know." Saniyah tried to console Reese before her cousin's emotion inspired more tears of her own.

"Well, I'm sorry all the same."

Reese's tone was low and defeated as she came to grips with the extent of her involvement in her cousin's misfortune. She realized that Ryan, even in the time she was with him, had shown no signs of being abusive, but her guilt outweighed her better judgment.

Saniyah heard the self-pity building in Reese. She did not want the joy of her emancipation to be spoiled by the unnecessary down pour of sadness. Knowing her cousin's love of a good laugh, she used humor to lighten the mood.

"It's all good, Cuz. Now, can you please come get me from this hospital before I catch mad cow from all these sick people up in here?"

The joke brought a smile to Reese's face, but she felt it was a mechanism for Saniyah to hide her feelings.

"Not until you tell me you forgive me."

Reese spoke with stern sincerity. After her painful break up with Andre, she was determined to cherish the relationships she had left.

"You're forgiven."

Saniyah respected Reese's sincerity with a genuine tone of her own. She appreciated her cousin's need for forgiveness. Although she felt Reese had done no wrong, it showed her loyalty.

"You still love me?" The sappy request for affection oozed from Reese's playful pout.

"Of course."

Simultaneous smiles graced both women's faces as they relished the reformation of the bond they had been losing to their relationships with men.

"I love you, too, Girl."

Saniyah stood in front of the door she had limped out of just a day ago. The pain and fear of her altercation were still fresh, but she knew it would not be long before Ryan took her absence out on her belongings. Backed by Reese, she unlocked the door with the key she never planned to use again.

Before entering the apartment, Saniyah called Ryan's name. Her call echoed through the space and went unanswered. She reluctantly crossed the threshold, and Reese eagerly rushed ahead of her.

"Girl, he ain't in here. Let's get this over with."

Reese motioned for her cousin to speed up her dragging feet. She walked into the bedroom and immediately surveyed the area for Saniyah's things. Saniyah started to walk in the bedroom's direction but froze as a vision of herself helpless and pleading in Ryan's clutches appeared against the kitchen wall. Fear shot through her paralyzed body and seemed to intensify the throb of pain in her side. She suddenly wanted to be a million miles away from the condo of horrors.

Retrieving her things was no longer important. She twisted back toward the exit so abruptly she had to grab her side to brace her injuries for the shock of the sudden movement. She grimaced in pain as she carefully wobbled toward the door.

"Where you goin'?"

Reese's question stopped Saniyah in her tracks. She maneuvered around to face her cousin's curious stare.

"I can't be here. I'm not ready. Can we do this another time?"

"Yeah, Niyah, whatever you want."

Reese saw the concern on her cousin's face and the apprehension in her posture. She walked over to Saniyah and pulled her into a warm embrace. Saniyah's tense body relaxed in the safety of her cousin's arms.

"Let me get the stuff I already packed. We can always come back for the other stuff when you're feeling better." Reese released her cousin and gave her a sympathetic smile before returning to the bedroom to retrieve the half-packed bag she left on Ryan's bed.

Saniyah immediately tried to emulate her cousin's touch with her own arms. She wrapped them around her shoulders and rubbed her skin to generate a soothing shield of warmth around her frigid fear.

Reese walked back into the living room with a Nike gym bag hanging across her chest.

"Wait, Reese, that's Ryan's bag. I don't think we should take it."

Fear shot back through Saniyah's body as she imagined the fit Ryan would throw if he knew they had taken something of his.

"Fuck him. He can buy another one."

Saniyah smiled at her cousin's matter-of-fact insult. Reese joined her in a liberating laugh, but their girl power moment was cut short when they heard the jiggle of a key in the doorknob.

Ryan walked into the uncomfortable silence aimed at him by both women. He looked at them curiously, pondering the reason for their presence. Coming home to an empty apartment after their fight, he hadn't expected to hear from Saniyah for a while. But when he spied his gym bag hanging off of Reese, he quickly deciphered the motive behind their visit.

"I guess you call yourself leaving me again, huh?"

Ryan stared down Saniyah's fragile eyes with his menacing intimidation. She shied away from his stare and remained silent.

"You damn right she's leaving. And she ain't coming back this time." Reese barked and stepped between Ryan and Saniyah.

"I wasn't talking to you."

Ryan's piercing focus shifted from Saniyah's cowering frame to Reese's confident scowl.

"Well, I'm talking to you."

Reese placed her hands on her hips and stood firm in her stance to show she was not backing down.

"Niyah, Baby, can we please talk about what happened? Don't just leave without giving me a chance to apologize."

"Apologize?" Reese sucked her teeth. "Nigga, you can apologize all day long, but it ain't gonna make up for putting her in the hospital."

"Hospital?"

Ryan looked to Saniyah for confirmation to Reese's revelation which she gave with a simple nod. Ryan was astonished that his anger had gotten so out of hand. His fit of rage had blinded him that night, and he could not remember the extent of the damage he had done. Guilt and shame took over his emotions but were short-lived before they were replaced by annoyance with Reese.

"Yeah, Nigga, your ruthless ass put her in the hospital this time. But there ain't gonna be a next time."

"Look, Reese, this don't concern you."

"Oh, but it does, Boo Boo. In case you forgot…this my family."

Reese reached for Saniyah and the cousins joined hands.

"You hurt her…you hurt me. And I don't like pain."

The strength and confidence in Reese seemed to transfer through her hand and into Saniyah because she suddenly felt able to handle the situation on her own.

"It's cool, Reese. Let me hear what he has to say."

Reese gave her cousin a curious stare, but backed out of the conversation when she saw the sincerity in Saniyah's nod. She walked over to the couch and plopped down into its cushions.

Ryan took Saniyah's hands in his and tried to pull her close, but she resisted. She locked her arms to keep her distance. Ryan respected her need for space but tightened his grip on her hands to keep the bond between them.

"Baby, I am so sorry I let this happen. I don't know what's wrong with me. But I promise to get some help to change. Just, please, don't leave me." Ryan pleaded with puppy dog eyes.

"Why? 'Cause you can't live without me?" Saniyah mimicked the excuse he gave in their last make-up session.

"Yeah, Boo. I need you." Ryan continued to grovel, misinterpreting the intention of her words.

"Do your other chick know that?"

"Forget her. I wanna be with you…just you."

"Look, Ryan, I heard all this shit before. I'm happy you wanna get help for your problems. But you need to do that for yourself, not me 'cause I'm done."

Saniyah snatched her hands out of his grip and turned away from his pleading pout.

"That's right, Cuz. You don't need this shit no more."

Reese popped up from her seat and rushed to her cousin's side, examining Ryan with a look of hatred.

"Reese, you can't even talk with all the bullshit you put your men through. Maybe if Andre would've put his foot in your ass, you'd know how to act."

"*Wow*!" Saniyah shook her head in disbelief. "So that's you trying to change, huh?"

"No, I was just..."

"Save it, Ryan."

Saniyah held her hand to his face to halt his explanation and kept it there to speak her mind without interruption.

"You know, I actually thought about going back to you this time. I thought about trying to help you become the better man I deserve. But I see now that you are who you are, and you ain't never gonna change. So I know I'm making the right decision."

Saniyah lowered her hand out of Ryan's sight and looked him straight in the eye.

"You and me are over. Don't come to see me, don't call me, don't even think about me 'cause I won't be thinking about you."

"But, baby, listen..."

Saniyah again silenced Ryan's begging with an outstretched palm. She took Reese's hand in hers and felt empowered and free.

"Reese, let's go. We'll get my stuff later." Saniyah and Reese walked hand in hand around Ryan's defeated frame toward the door. Saniyah grabbed the knob but suddenly remembered the huge ego and fragile pride of the man she was leaving behind.

"Ryan..."

Saniyah paused. Ryan turned his face slightly to acknowledge her call.

"I got a good ass lawyer so I suggest you keep your hands off my shit."

Made in the USA
Columbia, SC
04 November 2022

70446373R00147